by

Kathi Daley

This book is a work of fiction. Names, characters, places, and incidents either are products of the author's imagination or are used fictitiously. Any resemblance to actual events or locales or persons, living or dead, is entirely coincidental.

Copyright © 2015 by Katherine Daley

Version 1.0

All rights reserved, including the right of reproduction in whole or in part in any form.

Chapter 1

I'm not sure how I knew that the man sitting in the rusty old pickup truck was dead, but somehow I just did. Maybe it was the angle of his head, the tingling in my spine, or the likelihood that, I, Zoe Donovan, dead body magnet, would fall knee deep into a murder investigation seven days, eleven hours, twenty-three minutes, and seven seconds, before I was destined to become Mrs. Zachary Zion Zimmerman.

It was early in the morning and there were few vehicles on the road. My dog Charlie and I had been out jogging when we noticed the truck parked in front of Willy's Bar. Seeing a car parked in front of the bar wasn't in and of itself all that odd. There were occasions, I was certain, when a patron would have one too many and opt to leave their vehicle and get a ride home at the end of the night. It probably even wasn't all that odd to find a vehicle parked in front of the bar with a person sleeping it off inside. I almost continued on, but there was a little voice in my head that urged me to take a closer look.

I wiped the sweat from my brow with the back of my arm before Charlie and I made our way across the deserted street. I felt my heart begin to race as I approached the parked vehicle. You'd think I'd be used to this by now, but somehow, in spite of the ever-increasing number of dead bodies I seem to forever be stumbling across, I can't seem to control the momentary terror I always feel as I confirm what I know in my gut to be true.

I knocked on the driver's side window just in case my instinct was wrong and the guy was simply sleeping. When the man didn't move I tried the door, which fortunately—or unfortunately, depending on how you looked at it—was unlocked. The first thing I noticed upon opening it was the empty whiskey bottle on the seat. The man wore filthy clothing, but he didn't appear to have any blood on him, nor was there any evidence of foul play. Maybe the guy, whose face was concealed by a huge cowboy hat, really was just drunk.

"Hello," I said as loudly as I could without actually screaming in his ear.

The guy didn't move.

I reached out my hand to feel for a pulse.

There was none.

I removed the hat from the man's head, which caused that scream I'd been trying to avoid. Staring back at me with lifeless eyes was Pack Rat Nelson. Pack Rat, so nicknamed due to his propensity for collecting *everything*, lived in a run-down cabin outside of town, but he spent much of every day in the alley behind the shops on Main Street, collecting treasures from the Dumpsters that lined it. He seemed to always get around on foot and I'd never seen him drive, so I had to wonder how he'd come to be sitting in the cab of this particular truck.

Charlie and I called Sheriff Salinger and then waited for his arrival on a nearby bench. We'd only just finished up the murder investigation of the assistant to the wedding planner my future mother-in-law had hired the previous day. What were the odds that I'd stumble across another murder victim so soon?

If you know me at all you know the answer to that question is *pretty good*.

Of course I wasn't certain Pack Rat had been murdered. I hadn't moved the body, and so far I hadn't seen any blood. I didn't know Pack Rat all that well, but the guy seemed harmless, and he was well liked by the merchants he came in contact with on a daily basis despite his unique hobby.

"Do you think that truck belongs to Pack Rat?" I asked Charlie.

My dog tilted his head to the side, as if considering my question. One of the very best things about my furry best friend is that he really tries to appear interested in my rambling whether he understands what I'm saying or not.

"Maybe he borrowed it?"

Charlie barked as if he agreed with my assessment.

"And what is up with that hat?"

Charlie placed his paw on my thigh.

"Yeah. He probably just found it while he was out treasure hunting and decided to play cowboy."

While the hat was an unusual choice for Pack Rat, I felt its presence on his person could be explained. The bottle on the seat bothered me, though. While Pack Rat made a living recycling other people's garbage, he wasn't homeless, and although I wasn't all that close to him, I was fairly certain he wasn't a drunk. He lived in a three-room cabin on the edge of town that was packed with so many *treasures* you could barely get a body in the front door, but he seemed deliberate in his treasure collecting and had shared with me on more than one occasion that there wasn't a single item in his too-cluttered life he would consider parting with. If I had to guess, I'd say Pack Rat hadn't always lived off the land in quite the same way he chose to now. Although he was very rough around the edges, he seemed educated.

I was about to call Zak to let him know I'd be late getting home when Ellie called to ask about the plans we'd made for later in the day. Zak had offered to take his family who were in town sailing, and I'd invited my best friends, Ellie Davis and Levi Denton, to come along to act as a sort of buffer.

"Hey, Zoe. I hate to do this to you on such short notice, but Levi and I won't be able to make it today."

"I'm sorry to hear that." I sighed.

"I know you were counting on us, but we had a huge fight this morning and I really think we need to stay home to work things out."

Levi and Ellie had been best friends since kindergarten, but they'd only been a couple since Christmas. Things had been going so well for them until Levi had been offered a job four hundred miles away. Ellie owned a business and didn't want to move, but Levi was certain the opportunity he was being handed was too good to pass up. I couldn't see how this was going to work out without fractured friendships and broken hearts, but I'd prayed every day since I'd heard about the job that they'd find a way for them both to be happy.

"I'm sorry you're fighting," I answered. "I know this has been really hard on both of you. I agree; you need to talk this out. Besides, something happened, and I'm not sure we'll be going sailing anyway."

"Why? What's wrong?" I could hear the panic in Ellie's voice. "Are you okay? Is Zak okay? Oh, God, it's not the kids?"

"We're all fine," I assured my friend. "It's Pack Rat Nelson. He's dead."

"What? How?"

I knew Ellie used to save day-old bread and pastries for Pack Rat when she worked at Rosie's on Main, and like most of the merchants in town, while she didn't know him all that well, over the years she had grown to enjoy his visits.

"I'm not sure," I said. "I was jogging down the street and saw a man sitting in a parked truck. Somehow I just knew he was dead, so I crossed the street to investigate. I didn't move the body, but I didn't notice any sign of trauma."

"Wow. That's really too bad. I'm going to miss his tall tales and up-to-date gossip."

"Have you seen him lately?" I asked. Although Ellie's Beach Hut was down the beach from Pack Rat's usual route, it wasn't all that far of a walk. He often went by to see what sorts of goodies Ellie had saved for him.

"Yesterday I was busy rescuing you, so I didn't go into work, but I saw him on Thursday. Which is actually kind of odd because he usually doesn't come by on Thursdays."

"He has a regular schedule?" I asked.

"Yeah, as odd as it seems, he does tend to stick to a schedule. He normally stops by my place on Tuesdays and Saturdays. Although it does seem like he's been mixing it up the past couple of weeks. Maybe he was bored."

"Maybe. How did he seem when you saw him?" I asked.

"He seemed fine. I gave him some day-old doughnuts and a fresh cup of coffee to go with them. He seemed like he was in a good mood. He told me that he'd been down to the new development that's being built and had found a whole Dumpster full of treasures."

The new development Ellie spoke of was a somewhat controversial strip mall.

"The development is all the way on the edge of town. It seems like quite a way to get any treasures he might have found back to his cabin, which is on the other end of town."

"Maybe he borrowed the truck you found him in," Ellie suggested.

"Yeah. That's what I was thinking. Did he say anything else?"

"Just that he was going to head over to the Zoo to talk to Jeremy about a stray dog that's been hanging around in the campground."

I frowned. "Which campground?"

"I'm not sure," Ellie admitted. "Does it matter?"

"Probably not. It's just not like Pack Rat to turn in strays unless there's a problem with them."

"Now that you mention it, he did say it seemed like the dog was sick. Maybe you should ask Jeremy about it," she said, referring to my assistant at Zoe's Zoo, the wild and domestic animal rescue and rehabilitation shelter we run.

"Yeah, I will. Anything else?"

"He also said he saw Willa Walton arguing with some guy he didn't know in the parking lot outside the county offices. He mentioned that he didn't like the look of the guy. I asked him what he meant by that and he just said he had a small head."

"A small head?"

"Yeah. I guess it was too small for his body and that sort of creeped Pack Rat out."

I couldn't help but picture a man with a head the size of an eraser and the body of Superman.

"Salinger is just pulling up. If you think of anything else Pack Rat has talked about in the past week jot it down. We'll talk later."

"Do you suspect foul play?" Ellie asked.

"I always suspect foul play," I answered as Salinger opened the driver's side door of his squad car and got out. He was dressed in his sheriff's uniform, but it looked like he hadn't even stopped to comb his hair. It was early, but it wasn't that early. Our local sheriff must have had a late night.

"Do you have any idea what time it is?" Salinger grumbled as he wandered over to the bench where Charlie and I were waiting.

"Hey, I didn't kill the guy; I just found the body," I defended myself as I stood up to greet him.

"Any idea who he is?" Salinger asked as he looked toward the truck he had yet to approach.

"It's Pack Rat Nelson."

I could see by the look on his face that Salinger was surprised. "I didn't know he drove."

"He doesn't. Usually. I just spoke to Ellie, who last saw him on Thursday. She said he was excited about a bunch of stuff he found in the Dumpster over at the construction site of the new strip mall. We think he may have borrowed the truck to collect his treasure."

Salinger frowned and walked over to the truck. He looked inside and then pulled out his phone. I waited while he made a call to the morgue, requesting transport for Pack Rat. I knew he'd have additional questions for me once he'd arranged to have the body moved and the truck towed to the impound lot. I took out my phone to once again attempt to call Zak to fill him in on my delay getting home when he pulled up across the street.

"How'd you know I was here?" I asked after he jogged across the street and joined me.

"Ellie called me. Why didn't you?"

"I was going to, but then Ellie called, and before I could hang up with her Salinger arrived. Who's watching the kids?"

"Your dad is coming over. Are you okay?"

"I'm fine."

Zak took my hand in his and gave it a squeeze.

Maybe it was a delayed reaction to a life ended prematurely, or maybe it was just the emotion of finding the lifeless body of a man I knew, but suddenly I felt my heart constrict and my eyes tear up. I actually knew very little about the man I'd seen walking through town almost every day, but I knew enough to realize I'd miss him.

"The guy had a unique approach to life, but he seemed like a decent sort," Zak commented. "I often wondered how he ended up the way he did."

"I don't know. Maybe his lifestyle was nothing more than a simple choice. He seemed happy most of the time," I pointed out.

Zak looked toward the truck. "Do you know what happened?"

"No. Maybe Salinger will have some information once he's checked things out."

Zak put his arm around me and pulled me into his warmth. It felt so good to know I had someone I could lean on when life threw me curve balls. I hadn't always welcomed Zak's support, but now I didn't know what I'd do without it. I liked to pride myself on being an independent sort, but to be honest, now that Zak was in my life, I knew I could never live without him.

"Kind of odd that he's parked in front of a bar," Zak said.

"That's what I thought. He doesn't seem like the type to drink."

"He looks like someone who used to drink but has quit," Zak commented. "Unfortunately a lot of recovering alcoholics fall off the wagon at some point. I suppose that might be what happened."

"Yeah, maybe."

"One of my mom's uncles was sober for twenty-five years, and then one day he fell off the wagon for no apparent reason and drowned in the pond behind his barn," Zak informed me.

"That's really sad."

"The odd thing was that everyone who knew him swore he was in good spirits and seemed to have complete control of his drinking. His binge appeared to have been completely random."

"I guess we can never know what goes on in the minds of others, even those with whom we come into contact often."

Zak kissed the top of my head. "I suppose that's true. I certainly haven't been able to decode what goes on in your mind most of the time."

I smiled at him. "Oh, you're better at it than you think. It looks like Salinger is coming back this way."

Zak took a step back but kept a firm grip on my hand.

I watched the sheriff as he paused in the middle of the street and looked in both directions. He slowly turned in a circle, pausing to look at his surroundings as he did so. There was a two-story building on the opposite side of the street. Salinger shielded his eyes with one hand and studied the structure before continuing on across the street.

"Did you see anyone in the area when you arrived?" Salinger asked once he'd made his way to where Zak, Charlie, and I were waiting.

"No. The street was deserted."

"And you were walking along the sidewalk on this side of the street when you noticed the truck?"

"Jogging."

"What time would you say it was when you first arrived?"

I thought about it. "Six thirty-eight or, more accurately, a few seconds before six thirty-eight. I looked at my watch to check my pulse. That's when I noticed the man sitting in the truck and decided to check it out. When I realized he was dead I called you. And in anticipation of your next question, I didn't touch anything. Or at least not anything important. I opened the door, so you'll find my prints on the door handle. I also felt for a pulse and took off the hat he was wearing. After that I closed the door, came back across the street, sat down on that bench, and called you."

"Any idea who might want to harm Pack Rat?" Salinger asked.

"Not a one."

"Has he mentioned having an altercation with anyone? Maybe a dispute over the *treasures* he's collected recently?"

"Everyone I know really liked Pack Rat. He was kind of like a stray cat. He'd come around almost every morning to collect his treasures and the merchants along Main Street would offer him coffee, food, even money from time to time. I think the store owners looked forward to his visits. He usually had an interesting story to tell and he liked to chat with folks as he made his rounds."

"Yeah. That's what I thought."

"Ellie did mention that he was freaked out by a man Willa was speaking to. A man with a small head."

"A small head?" Salinger repeated my dubious comment.

I shrugged. "That's what she said. Oh, and she also mentioned that he'd been digging around in the Dumpster at the strip mall construction site. We suspect he may have borrowed the truck to collect whatever it was he found because he lives on the opposite end of town."

Salinger paused to look at the small notebook he was using to take notes. "The truck is registered to Orland Purlington. You ever heard of the guy?"

"No. Maybe he's a friend who lives out of town and Pack Rat took advantage of the fact he was here to collect his treasures."

"He's got a local address."

I looked at the truck that was parked along the curb. It was old and rusted through and I would be amazed if it even ran. It stood out like a sore thumb. It was odd that I'd never seen it before if the owner was a local. A truck in the particular state of disrepair as the one in which Pack Rat died would be hard not to notice.

"When you moved the body did you see any sign of foul play?" I asked Salinger

"Not on the surface. We won't know for certain what happened until we get an autopsy done. While it's possible he died of natural causes, my money is on something else. Maybe something that was added to his whiskey, or maybe there are injuries we'll find once we get him on the autopsy table. Do you know if Pack Rat had a drinking problem?"

"No. In fact, as far as I know he didn't drink at all. He always seemed alert when I spoke to him. Zak thinks he might have been a recovering alcoholic."

"Yes, well, I guess that could explain the bottle on the seat." Salinger glanced back toward the truck and then looked at me. "Guess I'll track this Orland Purlington down to see what he has to say. If you think of anything else call me."

Chapter 2

After we finished speaking to Salinger, Zak, Charlie, and I headed home. There really wasn't anything we could do at that point, and while I felt bad for Pack Rat, I had guests to see to and a wedding to prepare for. Although my mom had been very helpful in moving the Zimmerman clan from the house I share with Zak to a rental house, there were still family functions that it would be rude of us not to attend. Prior to the family members moving down the beach there had been four Zimmerman relatives in residence.

Zak's mother, Helen, was a very assertive woman who had definite ideas about her son's wedding and wasn't afraid to steamroll over whomever she had to in order to make certain her wishes were taken into account. Prior to my own mother's intervention on my behalf, it had seemed like the woman was on track to completely ruin our special day. My mom had assured me that things were taken care of and Zak and I would be able to have the wedding we'd planned, but I'd yet to speak to Mother Zimmerman personally, so I wasn't quite ready to celebrate.

Zak's cousin Jimmy was also in town. He was a *very* good-looking man who, if rumor was to be believed, wasn't nearly as bright as he was gorgeous. Jimmy, the eldest cousin of the group, was thirty-six, the eldest son of Helen's older brother Thomas. Jimmy had two younger brothers who planned to attend the wedding but weren't scheduled to arrive until the Friday before the event.

Eric was the only cousin who wasn't a Zimmerman by birth, and the only cousin who was married. He's thirty-two and had originally arrived with his wife Cindy, but they'd had a blowout over Eric's philandering ways and Cindy had left Ashton Falls a few days earlier. Eric was the only child of Helen's younger sister Wanda. Helen and Wanda had suffered a falling out years before, and according to what I'd learned from Cindy, she didn't plan to come to the wedding. Eric's grandmother, however, a woman I'd heard referred to as *a real character*, did plan to come and was scheduled to arrive later in the week.

And, finally, Zak's youngest cousin, a seventeen-year-old named Darlene, seemed to be the only visiting relative actually having fun. Darlene was the younger daughter of Helen Zimmerman's youngest brother, Joseph. Her older sister Twyla, mother to the progeny Helen had thought were going to participate in the wedding as ring bearer and flower girl, was scheduled to arrive next Thursday. I hoped my mom had been able to firmly convince Mrs. Zimmerman that Scooter and Alex were going to serve in those very important roles.

For any of you who may not know, Scooter is a ten-year-old boy Zak had befriended and mentored and Alex was a ten-year-old girl who went to the same boarding school Scooter attended. Both children are staying with Zak and me until after the honeymoon, which we'd planned to turn into a family vacation.

"Before we meet my family at the boat I think I need to warn you about a couple of things," Zak said as we loaded the SUV for a day of sailing.

I groaned. "What kind of things?" After all that had happened already, if Zak was giving me an additional warning it was going to be bad.

"My mother's best friend, Susan, arrived this morning with her daughter, Isabella. From the moment Isabella and I were born only five days apart my mom and Susan had been planning on the two of us marrying. I want to assure you that there has never been anything between us other than friendship, but based on her behavior this week, I wouldn't put it past my mom to try to make our relationship appear to be more intimate than it is."

"Let me guess: Isabella is gorgeous."

"Drop dead," Zak confirmed.

I frowned.

"Just remember, I'm marrying you."

I smiled. "I know. I love you and I promise to leave jealous Zoe in the past. Thanks for the heads-up, though. Are there any other additions to the family unit that I should know about?"

"As far as I know, Mom, Jimmy, Eric, Darlene, Susan, and Isabella are the only people coming sailing today. It'll be fun. I promise. Alex told me that she's never been sailing, and Scooter is superexcited about bringing his friend Tucker."

Tucker was a precocious eleven-year-old who had been best friends with Scooter until he'd left Ashton Falls.

"I'm sure it will be a nice day." I tried for a genuine smile. "I'm looking forward to meeting your mom's friends."

Zak kissed me on the tip of my nose. "You're a terrible liar."

"Maybe, but I'm *your* terrible liar. What does Isabella do for a living?" I don't know why I cared, but I sort of hoped she was a clerk in a mini-mart rather than a lawyer or stockbroker.

"She's a software developer too, only she specializes in gaming."

"So in other words, you have nothing in common," I teased.

"Yeah. Something like that. Did you pack the sunscreen?"

"It's in the bag with the beach towels. Have you ever worked on a project with Isabella?"

Zak shrugged. "Yeah. A time or two. It was after I sold my company but before I moved back to Ashton Falls. Did you remember glasses for the wine?"

"In the blue-and-green–striped bag. So you developed a game together?"

"Yeah, I guess you could say that. Isabella doesn't eat red meat. Did you bring any of that ahi I set aside?"

"It's in the ice chest. Which game?" I asked.

Zak stopped what he was doing and looked at me. I could see he was hesitant to say. This couldn't be good.

"It was just a game."

"And does this game have a name?" I really didn't know why I was pushing, but it seemed odd that he wouldn't just come right out with it.

"Zombie Slayer."

"Isabella wrote Zombie Slayer?" Zombie Slayer was my favorite video game. Or at least it had been until now. "You co-wrote Zombie Slayer? Why haven't you told me that before?"

"I don't know. It never came up. Do you think we should make a couple of peanut butter sandwiches for the kids? Kids love peanut butter."

"I made tuna for the kids. They all said they liked tuna. So I guess you and Isabella must have spent a lot of time together while you were writing the code for Zombie Slayer."

Zak shrugged. "I guess. But remember, we spent time together as friends."

"Friends with benefits?"

Zak turned to look me in the eye. "Just friends. I promise."

I smiled. "Okay."

"Can we waterski today?" Scooter walked up and tossed an armload of beach toys into the back of the SUV.

"We're going sailing," Zak reminded him. "I'll take you waterskiing later in the week. And I'm afraid we won't need this Super Soaker or football either." Zak handed the items back to Scooter.

"We aren't going to land on the beach?"

"Sorry, buddy. This is a sailing-only excursion. Maybe tomorrow."

Scooter sighed. "Okay."

"And remember, today is one of those best-behavior occasions," Zak reminded him.

"I remember. When are all of these people going home?"

"After the wedding," Zak answered.

"Weddings are boring. I'm never getting married."

Zak smiled. "Yeah, well, we'll see how that works out."

Zak and I were relaxing on the deck overlooking the lake later that evening after the kids had gone to bed. The moon shone down on the lake as the hum of the pool filter filled the still air. In spite of the fact that Isabella was gorgeous and a natural flirt and a genius software developer who just happened to have developed my favorite video game, it had turned out to be a nice day. Even the kids seemed to have had fun even though it was a sailing-only excursion.

"I was thinking, now that we agreed to BBQ here tomorrow, I'll invite my parents, Levi, Ellie, and maybe Grandpa and Hazel," I said.

"Sounds good. I wanted to catch up with Levi anyway. He's been bugging me about a bachelor party that I really wasn't planning to have."

"Yeah, Ellie's planning a small bachelorette party for me. I know it's a tradition, but I don't have the energy for a huge party. I think we've agreed to no more than eight women at the boathouse on Tuesday evening for a BBQ. Maybe you, Levi, and a couple of guys can do something the same night," I suggested.

"I guess that would be okay. If we do it on the same night, though, what are we going to do with the kids?"

"I'll ask my parents to have them over for a few hours. If you do something be sure to invite Jeremy," I said.

"I will."

I took a sip of my wine as a warm breeze brushed my shoulders. It was nights like this that convinced me I would never leave my mountain home. Although I'd lived in the same small town my entire life, I couldn't imagine living anywhere else.

"I'm glad Scooter and Tucker are having such a good time this weekend," I offered, "but I suspect Alex feels left out. I thought I'd take her shopping in the morning if you don't mind hanging out with the boys. She's really excited about our trip to Heavenly Island and I thought it would be fun to buy her some new clothes to bring."

"I don't mind hanging out with the boys at all. I think it's nice you want to have some girl time with Alex."

"Your mom thinks I'm using her as a surrogate."

"What? What are you talking about?"

"Today. On the boat. She mentioned to me that you'd talked to her about us taking the kids with us on the honeymoon we'd planned rather than the one she purchased for us. I could tell she was both hurt and angry that we weren't thrilled about her gift, but I explained that the kids were only going to be with us for a short time and we wanted to spend as much of it with them as we could. She made a comment about us having our own children rather than using other people's children as some sort of surrogate."

"My mother doesn't understand how we can love these two wonderful kids who have become such a big part of our lives even though they aren't our own. She focused all her attention on me from the moment I was born. I don't think she understands the concept of making room in our lives for children who don't share our blood."

"I tried to explain the relationship we have with Scooter and Alex, but she just kept insisting that once we have our own baby we'll forget all about them. We won't, will we?"

Zak took my hand and squeezed it. "Absolutely not. Those kids are going to be stuck with us for as long as they'll have us. Scooter told me he asked his grandparents if he can come for Christmas again."

"I'd like that, but I'll understand if they want to spend time with him as well. Have you heard any more about what's going on with his dad?"

When Scooter's mother died his dad had a mental breakdown of sorts and Scooter was basically left to his own devices. Roaming the town unattended, he was heading for a life in the criminal justice system until Zak befriended him and changed his life's trajectory. Scooter was now enrolled in a boarding school he loved, and while he did spend time with his grandparents on their farm, he spent quite a bit of time with us as well. His dad, however, had left Ashton Falls and hadn't been a real part of Scooter's life ever since.

"Scooter said his grandmother spoke to him. It seems he got a job and is doing okay, but he still doesn't show any interest in spending time with his son. Of course Scooter is hurt by it, but he's also happy there are no roadblocks to his spending time with us."

"I feel so bad for him, but I'm glad he's able to spend time with us this summer, and I do hope he can come for Christmas. Alex too, if her parents are still out of the country."

"I had a conversation with Alex earlier about her parents' project," Zak informed me. "The dig they were working on in the Middle East is wrapping up and they plan to head to South America next. The South American project is a two-year commitment, but it will be easier for them to arrange visits with Alex, though she did hint that she'd much prefer spending Christmas in Ashton Falls than in the jungle, so I suppose I'll e-mail her parents to see what their thoughts might be on the subject."

"It's so odd to me that her parents would even consider letting her spend Christmas with us, but from what Alex has shared it seems that arranging visits on her school holidays is really more of a hassle than an opportunity."

"They definitely have a unique perspective on child-rearing."

I sat back and closed my eyes. The pool filter had clicked off, so I could hear the frogs in the distance. I loved spending time on the lake during the summer months. There's nothing better than living in a place where the water meets the forest and the forest meets the sky.

"My mom asked me today about our plans for a rehearsal dinner."

"I thought we decided we didn't really need to have a rehearsal," I reminded Zak.

"We did, but she's insisting it's a tradition to have a dinner for the wedding party, relatives, and out-of-town guests on the night before the wedding. I thought we might come up with a compromise."

"What sort of compromise?" I asked.

"Maybe we can do something on Thursday, or maybe we can have a rehearsal lunch on Friday," Zak suggested. "That way we can still have the quiet evening we hoped for on Friday."

"I guess that would be okay," I grudgingly agreed. "Who knew getting married would be so much work?"

"Wedding planning has been a lot more of a challenge than I anticipated." Zak laced his fingers through mine. "Are you getting nervous?"

Was I? I certainly thought I'd be frantic by now. The old Zoe had major commitment issues, but the new-and-improved Zoe couldn't wait to become Zoe Donovan Zimmerman.

"No, not nervous. I'll admit I'll be glad when we can settle back into our regular lives. I feel like my schedule is all messed up, and while I don't think I'm exactly OCD, I do appreciate a routine of sorts."

"I guess it's normal to feel most comfortable when your life follows a predictable routine," Zak agreed.

I frowned. When Zak said the words *predictable routine* it jogged a memory.

Zak looked at me. "Something on your mind? You got real quiet all of a sudden."

"Ellie said Pack Rat's routine has been off the past couple of weeks. I wonder if that's relevant."

"What do you mean?" Zak asked.

"She mentioned that he was by her place on Thursday, which was odd because he normally visited the Beach Hut on Tuesdays and Saturdays. She indicated that he had a regular schedule he adhered to, but it had been off the past couple of weeks. Why would it have been off?"

"You think whatever interfered with his schedule could be behind his death?"

"I don't know. Maybe. It seems like an interesting enough idea to check out further."

"You're going to investigate Pack Rat's death."

"I'm not going to *investigate*," I insisted. "I'm just going to follow up on a hunch."

"We have guests to entertain."

"I know. I can do both. I think I'll go in and call Ellie to see if she knows more about his routine."

Zak reached over and pulled me onto his lap. He kissed my neck on both sides before finding my lips.

"Or maybe it can wait until tomorrow," I mumbled as I felt my body melt into Zak's.

Chapter 3

The next morning I got up early to find Alex sitting at the kitchen table writing in a black book that looked like a journal. She was so intent on her endeavor that she didn't even notice my presence. I'm not sure I'd ever seen quite that level of intense concentration on the face of a ten-year-old before. She bit her lower lip as she jotted something down, paused for a moment, and clicked her pen open and closed several times in rapid succession before continuing on with the next note.

"You're up early," I commented as I continued into the room and turned on the coffeemaker.

"I wanted some quiet time to write in my diary before everyone got up." Alex closed the book and fastened the small gold lock.

"I didn't know you kept a diary," I said to the dark-haired girl.

"I started after I found Addie's diaries when I was here at Christmas. I realized what a wonderful thing it was that she wrote down the details of her life so that someone who lived long after she died could read them."

"That's wonderful," I said as I poured myself a cup of coffee and sat down across from her. "I've considered keeping a journal myself, but I've never had the discipline to actually stick to it. I guess maybe it isn't my lot in life to be a writer."

"I love to write." Alex smiled. Her blue eyes sparkled with enthusiasm. "In fact, I'm writing a novel."

"You are?" I was surprised. Alex was the most intelligent and mature child I had ever met, yet she *was* just ten.

"Phyllis is helping me."

Phyllis King, a retired English professor, had taken an interest in Alex when she visited us in December. I knew both she and librarian Hazel Hampton had been sending her books since then, but I had no idea they were working on a project together.

"I write a chapter and e-mail it to Phyllis, and then she makes some notes and sends it back. It's been so much fun."

"I'd love to read your book."

A look of panic came over Alex's face.

"When you're ready to share it, that is," I said quickly.

Alex let out a deep breath. "I want you to read it. When it's done. Right now it feels kind of personal, if you know what I mean."

"I absolutely know what you mean," I assured the girl. "Can you at least tell me what it's about?"

"It's about a girl who goes to boarding school and makes some really awesome friends, and they have all of these wonderful adventures."

"Kind of like you," I pointed out.

"No. Not like me. Other than Scooter, I don't really have a lot of friends at school, and other than coming to see you and visits with my parents, I don't really have any adventures. Sure, I've been to a lot of different countries with my parents, but they were academic trips, not really adventures."

I frowned. "You don't have a lot of friends?" I couldn't imagine that was true. Alex was such a friendly and terrific person.

"It's not like anyone is mean to me or anything; it's just that I don't have a lot in common with the kids in my school. The girls who share a dorm room with me are ten like I am, but they were in the fourth grade last year, while I was taking eighth-grade classes. I think most of the girls think of me as some sort of brainiac freak. And maybe I am. I know we certainly didn't have anything in common."

"But you have something in common with Scooter?" I thought of the boy who blew milk

31

bubbles out of his nose last night at dinner and was most proud of his ability to burp the alphabet.

"Sure. Scooter's fun. He's not pretentious or complex. He's just Scooter. He doesn't care that I'm smart and I don't care that he isn't. We have fun together. He's even helping me with the book."

"He's helping you write it?"

"Well, he doesn't actually do any writing," Alex admitted. "But he has a wonderful imagination, and he helps me come up with adventures for my characters to go on."

"And the kids in your class?"

"They were so much older than me. I know it's only a couple of years, but there's actually a big difference between ten and thirteen. They're usually nice to my face, but I hear them calling me a baby behind my back."

"Oh, honey. That's awful."

Alex shrugged. "It's okay. I don't really want to hang out with any of them anyway. My parents are talking about transferring me to a high school next year, so any friendships I would have made would have been temporary anyway."

"They want you to go to high school?" I clarified. The girl was brilliant, but she was still a kid. If she didn't have anything in common with her classmates the year before, it would be even worse in a school filled with teenagers.

Alex nodded. "There's a boarding school north of the one Scooter and I attend now that caters to students with high IQs. They usually only take students who are between fourteen and eighteen, but my parents are trying to get them to make an exception for me. I aced all of my classes last year and eighth is the highest grade that school has, so there really isn't anywhere for me to go unless I transfer."

I thought transferring her to a high school was a horrible idea, but I didn't want to upset the child, and it really wasn't any of my business anyway. Surely there were other students her age who were close to being as advanced as she was who she could attend classes with.

"So how do you feel about transferring?" I asked.

"Honestly? I'm terrified. I know it's the best move for me academically. My parents and counselor agree on that. But I'm not ready for dating and high school parties. I know I won't fit in, but I'm not sure there are any other options."

"There's always homeschooling and private tutors."

"In order to be homeschooled you have to have a home." Alex placed her hand over mine. "Don't worry about it. I'll be fine. I always am."

I felt like I was going to cry, so I changed the subject.

"Are you still up for some shopping today? I feel the need to shop till I drop."

"Can we have lunch in town as well?"

"Absolutely."

I'd never been much of a shopper, but buying clothes for Alex to wear on our trip turned out to be the most fun I'd had in a long time. For one thing, the girl was *sooo* appreciative of every single item we purchased. For another, bringing a smile to her face warmed my heart in a way that was totally different from the way my soul had been touched by anyone else.

"Pink or green?" Alex asked, holding up an adorable sundress. Her blue eyes sparkled with enthusiasm as she presented the choices.

"Personally, I like the green, but it's your dress, so pick the color you like the best," I answered.

"I like the green." Alex smiled. "Maybe we can go back and buy those green sunglasses we saw in the shop we looked in just before this one. If I remember right, they'd match the dress perfectly."

"Oh, they would match. And they had matching flip-flops too. You're definitely going to be the best-dressed ten-year-old on Heavenly Island."

Alex grinned.

"I think we should buy you a couple of bathing suits, and some shorts and tank tops for the beach. They have a rack in the back of the store that has some cute options," I added. "Why don't you get started and I'll put this with the others."

"Are you sure that isn't too much?"

"I'm sure."

I took the dress we'd picked out for Alex and headed toward the front counter, where the clerk was keeping our selections. I was about to head back to the area where the bathing suits were kept when Phyllis King and Hazel Hampton came in through the front door.

"Morning, Phyllis, Hazel," I greeted.

"Zak told us you were shopping with Alex. Is she here? We've been so excited about her visit we couldn't wait another day to see her."

I suppose I shouldn't have been surprised by Phyllis and Hazel's level of enthusiasm, but I was. Still, Alex did share a love of books and reading with both women, so it made sense.

"She's in the back of the store. I was just heading in that direction. We're picking out bathing suits."

"I hope you don't mind if we intruded on your day," Phyllis apologized.

"Not at all. In fact, you should join us for lunch. We're going to Ellie's after we finish up here."

"I'd like that very much," Phyllis answered, and Hazel nodded her agreement. "It's such a nice day for lunch on the wharf. I spoke to Ellie a few days ago and she said business is booming."

"I know there's nowhere I'd rather have lunch than at the beach during the summer."

The two women followed me toward the back of the store. "I heard about Pack Rat," Hazel said. "I have to say I'm going to miss his biweekly visits."

"He spent time at the library?" I asked.

"He came in twice a week to check out a book and return the one he'd finished."

"Really? I know this is going to sound like a stereotype, but given his choice of occupation, I never pegged him as a reader."

"Pack Rat was actually very intelligent," Hazel confirmed. "I'm not sure why he went out of his way to conceal that. He always came in to chat for a minute and exchange his books at the very end of the day, when no one else was there."

I looked around for Alex, but I didn't see her, so I figured she must be in the dressing room.

I decided to check out my theory. "Did he always come in on the same two days?"

"Yes. Every Monday and Thursday. Like clockwork. Well, at least until the past few weeks. Something seems to have upset his schedule."

"Did he say anything that gave you an idea what that something might be?" I asked.

"No, and I didn't ask. I just noticed that he missed a Monday a few weeks ago and came on the following Wednesday, and then the next week he didn't come at all until Friday."

"What types of books did Pack Rat favor?" I asked.

"Oh, all types. Classics, thrillers, even Russian literature. It seemed like he was most interested in the history of Ashton Falls as of late."

"He was interested in the history of the area? Did he say why?"

"No. But it wasn't out of character for him to enjoy reading about historical events. He never would engage in a conversation about his own past before coming to Ashton Falls, but I don't think he was always a scavenger. If I had to guess I'd say he lived a fairly normal life until some great tragedy landed him here."

"You know, I had that same thought," I confirmed. "He was rough and he came across as uneducated, but there was something about him that just didn't quite sell his story. It's hard to understand what sort of event could cause a man to choose the life he did."

"I'm not certain, but I think he might have been in the military at one point," Hazel said. "He never said as much, but there was just something about his actions that reminded me of an old friend of mine who had seen heavy combat and never really recovered."

"Like what kind of actions?" I asked.

"One time I was sorting books when he came in. I dropped a heavy encyclopedia and it made a loud bang when it hit the tile floor. Pack Rat jumped and looked around like he expected the sound to have come from gunfire rather than a falling book. Of course I'm speculating. Loud noises do startle people, and I really don't know if he associated that sound with a gun or something else. It was just the fear in his eyes coupled with the thud of the book that reminded me of my friend."

"I suppose it makes sense that if he'd been involved in some sort of combat situation he might choose to retreat from living an ordinary life. If he did serve in the military I wonder which war."

Hazel shrugged. "I'm not sure. Based on his age, I'd guess Vietnam. Of course it seems as if there's always a war somewhere, and for all I know I could be way off about the military thing. It might have been something else entirely that had him spooked."

"You talked to him on a regular basis, so I'm wondering if you have any idea who might want him dead."

"He was murdered?" Hazel looked surprised. "I'd heard he had a heart attack."

"I don't know for certain he was murdered, but I have the sense his death wasn't due to natural causes. I thought I'd drop in to talk to Salinger later to see if he has the autopsy report back."

"You know. . . " Hazel began, then hesitated.

"What?" I encouraged.

"It's probably nothing, but I know Pack Rat was upset with Willa. I don't know what he was upset about, but he made a comment about her not being the person she seemed. I'm sure it was just some little tiff about vagrancy laws or something. It's true that while most of the merchants in town didn't mind the sight of Pack Rat digging through their garbage, technically it's against the law in Ashton Falls, and Willa does tend to be a stickler for the rules."

Ellie had told me that Pack Rat had seen Willa arguing with some guy with a small head in the parking lot of the county offices. If he wasn't mad about Willa's adherence to the rules, could Pack Rat's beef with her have something to do with that?

"When was it that he said he was upset with Willa?"

Hazel thought about it. "I guess it must have been Monday of last week. Although," Hazel considered, "maybe he was in on Tuesday rather than Monday. I can't say for certain, although I could pull up his file to confirm which day he was in if it's important."

"It may not be, but I've learned anything can be important in an investigation. I'll let you know."

"Hazel! Phyllis!" Alex had come out of the dressing room and screeched with delight when she saw who I was talking to.

"My, you've grown since Christmas," Phyllis said as she hugged the girl.

"Why is it that 'my, you've grown' is the first thing adults say when they haven't seen you for a while?" Alex asked.

Phyllis laughed. "I don't know. I suppose 'my, I've missed you' would be more appropriate."

Alex hugged Phyllis for a second time before moving over to hug Hazel. "I've missed you too. Both of you. I have so much to tell you."

"Phyllis and Hazel are going to come to lunch with us, so you'll have plenty of time to catch up," I promised. "Now let's take a look at that bathing suit to make sure it fits as it should."

Alex twirled around the store. "What do you think?"

Alex's grin was so big and her eyes shone with happiness. I found her enthusiasm to be infectious and was tempted to twirl around the store myself. There was something about being with Alex that touched my heart and nourished my inner child.

Chapter 4

After lunch Alex went with Hazel and Phyllis while I headed over to the sheriff's office. We agreed that I would pick Alex up at Phyllis's when I'd finished with Salinger. We still needed to buy a dress for her to wear to the wedding. I had three for her to choose from on hold at Country Cousins, so I hoped my chat with him wouldn't take too long.

I pulled into the parking lot of the county offices and was glad to see Salinger's squad car on-site. On any other Sunday, Salinger would probably be off and a deputy would be on duty instead, but with a suspicious death to investigate I'd suspected he might be working. Obviously, I'd been right.

The reception area was deserted so I headed down the hallway and knocked on his office door.

"Come in," Salinger called.

I opened the door.

"I've been expecting you."

"You have?" I asked.

"Figured you'd come snooping around looking for the inside scoop. I'm kind of surprised it took you this long."

I sat down in the chair across the desk. "I took Alex shopping or I probably would have been here earlier. So what do you know?"

"Quite a bit, actually."

Salinger paused to move some files around on his desk. I suspected his delay was simply a tactic to make me squirm while I waited for him to get to it. I decided I wouldn't give him the satisfaction of showing my impatience and simply smiled and waited.

For about two seconds.

"So?" I prompted.

"The man we know as Pack Rat Nelson died of heart failure."

"So he did die of natural causes?" I asked.

"Not necessarily. The coroner found a small puncture wound that appears to have been left by an injection in his neck. It was covered by his long hair and not immediately evident."

"So someone injected him with something that stopped his heart?"

"At this point that's what it looks like occurred," Salinger confirmed.

"Any idea what he was injected with?" I asked.

"The medical examiner believes it was air. They're running additional tests."

I knew that a large amount of air injected into the bloodstream would most likely result in death. What I didn't know was who would do such a thing to Pack Rat.

"Any idea at all who might have done it?" I asked.

"Not specifically. If the weapon was air in the circulatory system, I'd say we need to look at people with some level of medical knowledge. Whoever did this knew how much air to use and where to inject it. The killer would also have needed access to a hypodermic needle. I'm going to go out on a limb and say we're looking for a medical professional of some sort."

"Or a drug addict," I said.

"You make a good point. Focusing in on suspects who have access to needles and the knowledge required to kill a man via this particular method narrows the field a bit but not enough. We'll need more if we're going to solve this case."

I found that I liked the way Salinger was throwing around the word *we*.

"By the way, were you able to find out Pack Rat's real name?" I asked. "I'm certain it can't have been Pack Rat."

"That's my next bit of news. As of this moment we don't know who the man actually was. His fingerprints don't match any we have on file. In fact, they appear to have been intentionally altered. We're running a DNA test, but that could take a while. It seems he didn't have a driver's license or any other type of government identification."

"Okay, that's weird. Right?"

"Yeah. Weird. We're checking a few other sources. If we don't find anything we'll widen our search and circulate a photo."

I sat back in my chair and considered the situation. The tick tock of the old-fashioned clock on the wall counted down the seconds as I tried to make sense of what we knew. Pack Rat Nelson was a man without a name—at least a legal one—who died as a result of air being injected into his neck. Pack Rat wasn't a small man, so he probably hadn't seen his killer coming. Perhaps, as we'd suspected, he'd fallen off the wagon and tied one on the night he died and the killer had simply taken advantage of the fact that he was passed out in the truck parked in front of the bar.

"Did you check Pack Rat's blood alcohol level?" I asked.

"He hadn't had a drop."

"But the bottle on the seat?"

44

"We're dusting it for fingerprints. I'm not sure who drank the whiskey, but it wasn't Pack Rat."

"Did you speak to the man who owns the truck Pack Rat's body was found inside?" I asked.

"I did. He's out of state at the moment. He didn't know Pack Rat had borrowed his truck, but he did admit he leaves the keys over the visor, and Pack Rat knew that. It seems Pack Rat had borrowed the truck before when he needed to retrieve something large."

"There was nothing in the back of the truck," I pointed out. "If Pack Rat borrowed the truck to pick something up he either hadn't gone for it yet or he'd already picked it up, dropped it off at his place, and then headed back into town."

"I wonder what he was after," Salinger mused.

"Ellie told me he was excited about something he'd found in a Dumpster at the construction site for the new strip mall. That's a pretty good distance from his cabin. I guess he could have borrowed the truck to retrieve whatever he found."

"Maybe I'll have a talk with the contractors to see if anyone saw him at the site on the day he died," Salinger said.

"In the spirit of full disclosure," I added, "I ran into Hazel today, who said Pack Rat was upset with Willa Walton about something. Ellie also mentioned Pack Rat had told her he'd seen Willa arguing with a man with a small head. I don't know if either of those pieces of information are important, but I guess it wouldn't hurt for you to have a chat with Willa."

Thanks. I'll do that when she comes in to work tomorrow."

"Have you spoken to the people who work in the bar where the truck was parked?" I asked.

Salinger nodded. "The bartender on duty that night claims he didn't see anyone fitting Pack Rat's description. I spoke to several of the waitresses as well. Although he was parked in front of the establishment, it appears he didn't go inside."

"I wonder if he was with someone," I said. "Maybe he was sitting in the truck while his passenger went inside for a drink."

"If that were true you would think that person would have called me when he came out and found Pack Rat dead."

"Unless the passenger was the person who killed him."

I picked Alex up at Phyllis's and she and I went shopping for her flower girl dress. As I said earlier, I had three dresses on hold for her to choose from, but from the moment she laid eyes on the dress in the window, I knew our flower girl was going to be a princess.

"Have you ever seen such a perfectly perfect dress?" Alex breathed as she stood with her face plastered to the window.

It really was a beautiful gown. Sleeveless, with a silk underlay and a transparent skirt that was woven with threads of varying colors that seemed to change from blue to pink to silver as we studied the garment. The bodice was fitted but the skirt was full, giving the dress a fairy princess look.

"It really is perfect. I wonder if they have your size."

Alex turned to look at me with the most precious smile. "We can get it?"

"Sure. If they have your size and if you still like it when you try it on."

It did occur to me that with my simple wedding gown the flower girl was going to outshine the bride, but at that moment the last thing I had on my mind was being shown up by this adorable angel.

"I've never worn anything so beautiful. Do you think it's too much?"

"I think it's just right. Let's go inside to see what we can work out."

Alex really did look like Cinderella once she slipped into the magical dress—which, by the way, was one of a kind and just happened to fit her exactly. We bought her satin slippers to match and an ivory ribbon to weave through her hair. I had to physically fight back the tears as this wonderful child hugged me with all her might and thanked me for making her dreams come true.

When we left the dress shop we headed to the florist's to pick out the perfect flowers for my little princess to carry. Did I just say *my* princess? Yikes, I had it bad. My mothering instinct seemed to kick into overdrive whenever this very special little girl was near.

"You're so lucky to live somewhere with a beach," Alex commented as we walked along Main Street, which paralleled the lake on one side.

"Yeah, I do feel lucky to live here. I know you go to boarding school now, but where did you live before that?"

"Nowhere and everywhere."

"Wow. That's profound."

"I'm not complaining," Alex assured me. "It's just that when I was a baby my parents traveled. A lot. They still do, but back then they'd usually take me with them. I don't remember much from the early years, but by the time I turned four I know I thought it was perfectly normal to sleep in a tent at a dig one night and then a five-star hotel the next."

"So your parents have money?"

"My mom does. I think her parents are rich. They live in Boston."

"Do you visit with them often?" I asked as we turned the corner and headed toward Second Street, where the florist was located.

"Never. I mean, I've been to their place. A long time ago. I don't remember all that much except for endless hallways."

"Endless hallways?"

"I think I was about three the last time I was at their house. I remember there were these long hallways that seemed to lead one to another. The halls had dark burgundy carpeting and all the doors were painted in white. They kept the doors closed, so unless you knew where you were, one hallway looked just like all the others. I remember I got lost and sat down in the middle of one of those hallways and cried until someone came and found me."

"Oh, no. How terrifying. Who found you?"

"One of the maids. Her name was Ariel and she smelled like lemon. I think it was from the dusting oil, but ever since then I get warm feelings whenever I smell lemon. I was so scared and she was so nice."

I waved to Gilda Reynolds through the window of Bears and Beavers. Pam's Posies was wedged between Gilda's shop and Outback Hunting and Fishing. I opened the door and we walked inside. The store was cool in contrast to the heat of the afternoon and smelled like a fragrant garden in full bloom.

"So what kind of flowers should we order for you and Bella to carry?" I asked.

"You mean I can choose?"

"Absolutely. Anything you want."

She walked over to the floor-to-ceiling refrigerators with glass fronts and began to study the inventory. I greeted the proprietor, Pam, while Alex decided which flowers she liked the best.

"I'm surprised to see you here," Pam said. "I thought we decided to order daisies."

"The daisies are for me. Today we're shopping for Alex. She's the flower girl, along with Bella. I told her she could choose whichever flower she wanted to carry. I don't think Bella cares one way or the other."

Pam smiled. "Would you like me to help Alex choose a flower that will complement the bouquet you're going to be carrying?"

"No, let her choose what she wants. I don't care if we match. Most times I find matching to be overrated. Has Ellie been by to pick out her flowers?" I asked.

"Yes, she's all set. I have to say you have the most laid-back approach to the big day of any bride I've ever worked with."

I shrugged. "Flowers are just flowers. No offense."

Pam laughed. "No offense taken. I can appreciate your casual approach. I get a lot of brides who are completely manic about having the perfect flowers. Of course that's what keeps me in business, so I'm not complaining."

"You do an excellent job with your bouquets."

"I try. People seem to appreciate the extra care I put into every arrangement. I just hope it's enough."

"What do you mean?" I asked.

"I heard there's going to be a discount florist in that new strip mall. I'm afraid it's going to drive me out of business. I can't afford to sell my stock at the deep discounts the chains do."

"I'm sorry. I hadn't heard a florist was going in. If it helps at all, I can assure you that you'll have all of my business. Not that I buy a lot of flowers."

Pam smiled. It was a weak smile of defeat but a smile nonetheless.

"Can I have yellow roses?" Alex asked, wandering over.

"Yellow roses sound perfect. I think Bella will like them as well." I looked at Pam.

"I think I just happen to have yellow roses on order."

Alex grinned.

"Someone will be in on Friday to pick them up if that works for you," I said.

"I'll have them ready. If things get too hectic let me know and I'll deliver all the wedding flowers."

"Okay, thanks. I appreciate that."

We returned to the heat outside and I asked Alex, "So what should we do next?"

"Ice cream?"

"Ice cream sounds just about perfect."

Chapter 5

Although I knew Jeremy and Tiffany Middleton, our assistant, had everything under control at Zoe's Zoo, I decided I needed some time to gather my thoughts and gain perspective. The family BBQ the night before had turned into a three-ring circus that had me once again on the verge of running for the hills. Now that Eric's wife, Cindy, had left Ashton Falls, he was back to hitting on every female he came into contact with. Ellie almost smacked him when he *accidentally* grazed her breast, and when he tried the same move on me I accidentally on purpose spilled an entire pitcher of margaritas down the front of his pants. The guy was a complete and total lech who seemed to gain some sort of twisted pleasure from creating a response of revulsion from the women he hit on. I was having a very hard time believing my sweet and loveable Zak was related to the guy.

And then there was Isabella. Zak had assured me the two of them were just friends, and although she was an obvious flirt, she had seemed to keep her distance when we'd gone boating. But last night she'd dressed in the skimpiest outfit I'd ever seen and then proceeded to stick to Zak like a fly on flypaper. Zak was polite, and I could tell he was trying to maintain a reasonable distance, but every time he tried to walk away Isabella found an excuse to pull him back in.

"Rough night?" Jeremy asked when he walked into my office and found me nursing my third cup of coffee.

"The roughest."

"The Zimmerman clan still making your life miserable?"

"Not as much as they were before my mom found them new accommodations, but yeah. When Mrs. Zimmerman announced her plans to spend the morning at the house I decided to escape to the Zoo for a while. By the way, I've been meaning to ask if Pack Rat ever came in to talk to you about a stray dog in the campground."

"Yeah, he came in last week. I guess the dog had been acting oddly and he was concerned that it might be sick. I've been driving through the campground whenever I'm out doing my rounds, but I haven't seen it. I pinned a description of it, along with our phone number, on the bulletin boards near the bathrooms, but so far no one has called. It looks like either someone picked him up or he moved on."

"So we're talking about Babbling Brook Campground?"

"Yeah."

"And Pack Rat had seen this dog on more than one occasion?"

"Yeah. He made it sound like he'd seen it several times at least. Why?"

"It's just that the campground is at least three miles from town. I was just wondering why he was out there in the first place."

"He said a friend of his was staying there."

"Did he mention this friend's name?"

"No. Does it matter?"

"It might."

"Oh, I get it." Jeremy looked like a light just went on in his head. "You think the friend might know something about Pack Rat's death."

"I think it's a possibility. How is everything else going?"

"I found an awesome home for the little Corgi who was brought in a few weeks ago. When the man I'd spoken to on the phone brought his daughter in to meet the dog it was obvious to everyone that it was love at first sight for both the girl and the dog."

"I'm so glad. I was hoping we'd find a good placement for the little guy. Any luck with the pair of feline sisters we rescued from the kill shelter in Bryton Lake?"

"Not yet, but I'll find them the perfect home. It's going to be a little harder because they're both older and we want to place them together. Most people come in looking for kittens."

"Speaking of kittens, how are the newborns I rescued last week from the lumber mill?"

"They're doing well. They sure are fluffy for newborns. I bet they're going to be beautiful when they grow up."

"I'm glad I got to them before the coyotes who were stalking them did."

"Speaking of wild animals, I got a call from Fish and Game this morning. They've had two nuisance bear calls this week from merchants on Main Street. It seems we have a mama and cub who have developed a taste for Dumpster diving. Fish and Game did a couple of sweeps, but now that their office has moved off the mountain they're finding it hard to do regular sweeps. They asked if we could work out something with the merchants to call us when the bears are spotted."

"Most of the business owners already do call us if there's a problem. Who called in the complaints?"

"Jim's Taco Hut and that new bakery, Sprinkles."

"Okay, I'll head over to have a chat with both owners."

Jim's Taco Hut had been around forever, and although I'd spoken to, yelled at, threatened, and pleaded with the owner on numerous occasions to buy bear-proof containers or at the very least keep the lid on his Dumpster secure, he seemed to always find a reason for the dang thing to be left open. I had little hope of making any headway with the guy, but I felt I had to try.

Sprinkles, on the other hand, was a new business that might very well just not understand the importance of securing their yummy refuse. I figured I'd start with them before heading over to Jim's Taco Hut to butt heads with the totally clueless owner.

Walking into Sprinkles was like stepping into a children's fantasy. The bakery had only just opened the month before, and while I'd heard good things about the food, I'd yet to take the time to stop by. The shop was decorated in bright colors that really did remind me of candy sprinkles. I sat down on one of the pink bar stools and ordered a lemon cupcake with bright yellow frosting.

"I love your interior design." I smiled at the girl behind the counter.

"Thanks. I loved Strawberry Shortcake when I was a kid and wanted to re-create the feeling of living in a world filled with nummy goodness. I'm Kammy."

"Zoe," I replied.

"You own that animal shelter in town. I've been thinking about getting a playmate for Muffin now that I'm away from home so much."

"Muffin?"

"My dog. His sister, Cupcake, passed a few months back. Poor dear was devastated, but we hadn't opened yet and I was able to bring him to work with me. Now that we've opened I work long hours and the poor thing is home alone."

"If you're looking for a small dog we have several. You should come by to play with them. Maybe one will capture your heart."

"Can I bring Muffin? I wouldn't want to adopt a dog Muffin didn't adore."

"As long as Muffin is dog friendly and current on his shots, we'd love to have him come for a visit."

The girl, with long blond hair and deep blue eyes, smiled at me. "Thanks. You're okay. The cupcake is on the house."

I took a bite of the creamy frosting that melted in my mouth. "The main reason I stopped by," I added, "was to talk to you about the problem you've been having with the mama bear and her cub."

"You heard about that? Of course you heard about that. You run an animal shelter. The cub is really cute and all, but I'm a city girl born and bred, and I'm not used to coming face-to-face with wild animals."

"What exactly happened?" I asked.

"A few days ago I went out to dump the trash and heard rustling, so I decided to check it out. At first I thought it was that guy who digs around in everyone's garbage, but when I saw this huge ol' bear staring at me, I nearly peed my pants."

"The bears in our area are mostly harmless, but I wouldn't get between a bear and its lunch or a bear and its cub."

"Trust me, when I saw the mama bear and her cute little baby I came back inside, locked the door, and called Fish and Game."

"Calling F and G wasn't the wrong thing to do, but we find it usually works best to call the Zoo if you have a problem with either a wild or a domestic animal. We're closer and can usually respond in a timely manner." I handed the girl my card. "You can call this number any time. We have staff around the clock."

"I appreciate you taking the time to stop by to fill me in. I had no idea."

"I figured." I smiled. "If you really want to keep the mama and her cub from invading your garbage you should invest in a bear-proof Dumpster. They can be a little pricey up front, but a bear-proof can will keep the bears from hanging around at your end of the alley."

"There are bear-proof Dumpsters?"

I explained how the cans worked and gave Kammy the phone number for a company that built and installed them. It took a while to get through my entire spiel because customers wandered in and out the entire time we were talking. It looked like Sprinkles was going to be a huge success. I had to wonder how the other dedicated bakery in town felt about the new competition.

"By the way," I commented before I left, "the man you thought was in your garbage when you heard the rustling . . . were you referring to Pack Rat Nelson?"

"I don't know his name."

"He's a tall guy. Over six feet. Sort of stocky."

"Yeah, he's one of the scavengers I've seen. The other guy is short with one arm. I think he's new to the area. He just started showing up with the bigger guy a few weeks ago."

"And you didn't catch a name?" I asked.

"No. The men seemed harmless enough, and I've seen other merchants chatting with them, but I grew up in a neighborhood where you didn't speak to vagrants."

After leaving Sprinkles I headed over to Jim's Taco Hut even though I knew doing so was going to prove to be fruitless. I'd tried on numerous occasions to gain cooperation from the eatery's owner with zero success. Part of the problem was that Jim had this way of listening to you without really listening. He'd look you straight in the eye while you laid out all the reasons why investing in a bear-proof Dumpster was a good idea. When you had completed your explanation he'd pause and wait for you to ask him if he understood what you were saying. He'd swear he did and agreed with every word, but that would be the end of it. He never would get around to ordering the bear-proof can. We'd been dancing to the same tune for years now and not a single thing about his approach to garbage management had changed.

"Zoe, what are you doing responding to bear calls five days before your wedding?" Jim asked.

"It's my job to respond to bear calls. Do you want to tell me what happened?" I asked.

He did.

"I thought we talked about the fact that your open Dumpster attracts the bears," I reminded him.

He agreed that we had.

I went over the reasons why purchasing a bear-proof can would benefit not only him but the nearby businesses as well.

He acknowledged my argument.

"How about if I buy a bear-proof Dumpster and have it installed at no cost to you?" I offered.

Jim appeared to be considering my offer. An offer I'd made before without success.

"This means a lot to you?" he asked.

"It really does."

"I guess now that Pack Rat is gone it doesn't matter."

"What does this have to do with Pack Rat?" I wondered.

"I figured if the can was bear proof it would be rat proof. I kind of liked having the guy around."

I had to admit I was completely stunned. "You mean you've been fighting me on the bear-proof can all these years because you thought it would keep Pack Rat from rummaging around in your garbage?"

"The guy has to eat."

If the whole thing wasn't so ridiculous, and so sad, I would have laughed. I was about to point out the absurdity of Jim's statement but decided to let it go. The guy made pretty good tacos, but he wasn't known for his superior intellect.

"Can I assume that because Pack Rat is no longer with us you're okay with the bear-proof can?"

Jim shrugged. "Yeah, I guess. Heard you found the body."

"Yeah," I confirmed, "I did. One of the other merchants mentioned that Pack Rat had been hanging around with a short man with one arm. Do you know anything about that?"

"You must be talking about Stubby."

"Have Stubby and Pack Rat been friends long?" I asked.

Jim appeared to be thinking about it. "I guess Pack Rat first brought Stubby around a few weeks ago."

"Do you happen to know Stubby's real name?"

"Nope. Didn't ask. The guy has the look. I try to stay away from guys with the look."

"The look?"

"Puckered lips, shifty eyes that never really look at you directly. The man has a secret, I can tell you that. If I had to guess I'd say he's up to no good. I'm willing to bet he's most likely responsible for the rash of random burglaries some of the vendors have had as of late."

"Burglaries?"

"A handful of merchants along this block have had their businesses broken into the past couple of weeks, and if you ask me, they started about the time this Stubby character showed up."

I frowned. I hadn't heard about any burglaries. "Did you report this?"

"So far I haven't been a victim, but I don't think the others bothered making reports. Whoever is breaking in seems to just be taking small items without a lot of value. I suspected it might be Stubby, but the other merchants don't necessarily agree."

"Do you have any idea where this Stubby lives?"

"Nope."

"Will you call me if you see him?"

"Yup."

"Okay, thanks. I'll have someone come by to install your new bear-proof Dumpster this week."

I left Jim's Taco Hut and decided to head a few doors down the alley to Bears and Beavers to ask the store owner, Gilda Reynolds, if she knew anything about the man I now thought of as suspect #1. If Pack Rat had recently befriended a man with shifty eyes maybe this man was in some way responsible for his death. I'll admit there was a voice in my head reminding me that I was getting married at the end of the week, so perhaps this would be the time to take a step back and let Salinger handle the murder investigation, but we all know that particular little voice—the one I think of as the voice of reason—is the one I'm most apt to ignore.

"Morning, Gilda," I greeted her. Gilda is a short, stocky woman with bright red hair and a loud disposition. She runs the local theater group and is a member of the community events committee I participate in as well.

"Zoe." Gilda gave me a big hug. "I didn't expect to see you out and about with all the wedding planning I know you must be knee deep in the middle of."

"The wedding is pretty much planned, so I decided to go into work this morning. I'm actually here in regard to a nuisance bear call."

"There has been a mama and cub hanging around. Seem harmless. Who complained?"

I opened my mouth to speak.

"Let me guess," Gilda interrupted. "Jim at the Taco Hut. That man, and his total disregard for wildlife management practices, is what brings the bears to our alley in the first place."

"I spoke to Jim and he's finally agreed to a bear-proof container. I'm having one delivered this week. The reason I stopped by was to ask about Pack Rat."

"Heard what happened. Such a shame. Don't tell me you're investigating. You do know you have a wedding to prepare for."

"I'm aware I have a wedding coming up." Geez, how many mothers did I have in this town? "And I'm not investigating. Exactly. It's just that Jim mentioned that Pack Rat had been hanging around with another man. A short man with one arm. I was hoping you might know who he is."

Gilda set the box of bear-shaped mugs she had been inventorying on the counter. "I don't know his real name. Pack Rat introduced him as Stubby. I hadn't seen him hanging around before he showed up with Pack Rat a couple of weeks ago. My guess would be that he's just passing though."

"When was the last time you saw him?" I asked.

Gilda thought about it. "A few days ago. Wednesday or Thursday. He was lurking around the loading dock behind Outback Hunting and Fishing."

"Was Pack Rat with him?"

"I didn't see him."

"Jim indicated that some of the merchants on this block have been burglarized lately."

"Yeah. There are three or four of us that have noticed broken locks and missing items. The thefts seem random. I wouldn't have even noticed the missing items, but I saw that the lock on the door to the alley was bent, so I looked around and took a quick inventory. All that was missing were heavy socks with bears on them and a pair of moose salt and pepper shakers."

"I guess someone needed socks."

Gilda shrugged. "I guess. The others think it could be Stubby, but I kind of doubt it. He looks like the sort who would go for something of value."

"When did the break-in occur?" I asked.

"I noticed the broken lock when I came in on Monday of last week."

"Do you know who else was hit?" I asked.

"Second Hand Suzie's, for one."

"Do you know anything at all about this Stubby that might help me find him?"

"I thought you weren't investigating," Gilda pointed out.

"I'm not."

Gilda rolled her eyes.

Why is it that everyone thinks that just because I ask a few questions to assuage my curiosity I'm investigating?

"There's one thing I found curious," Gilda admitted. "It seemed like Pack Rat was almost afraid of Stubby."

"Afraid how?"

"I don't know. It was just a vibe. The first time he introduced Stubby he seemed nervous—like he really didn't want to introduce him but was compelled to do it. Stubby is shorter than I am and Pack Rat is a big guy, so the dynamic seemed off."

"You said the men had been seen together the past few weeks. Have they been together every time you've seen them?"

"No. Just that first time, and then again a day or two later I saw Stubby hanging out at Outback Hunting and Fishing. I don't have a lot of discarded items that Pack Rat might be interested in, so he doesn't come by my place as often as he visits some of the other stores. I know he shows up in the alley almost daily, but I rarely see him more than once a week. If you want to find out more about Stubby and his relationship with Pack Rat you might ask either Jim or Ernie."

Ernie Young owned the local market. I knew he gave expired bakery items and produce to Pack Rat on a regular basis.

"I spoke to Jim earlier, but I'll stop in to talk to Ernie. Thanks for the information."

"If someone hurt Pack Rat I hope you find them. That guy was a real decent sort."

When I went by the market Ernie wasn't in. The clerk told me that he wasn't expected back for a couple of hours. I really wanted to speak to Suzie at Second Hand Suzie's and Horton at Outback Hunting and Fishing, but it was getting late and I knew I should get home to face whatever pre-wedding plans were on the schedule for today. Meeting with Ernie and the others was going to have to wait for another day.

Chapter 6

When I walked in the front door and saw that the entire Zimmerman clan had descended on casa Zimmerman, I almost turned around and walked back out. Scooter and Alex were in the pool, Darlene and Jimmy were sunbathing, Eric was sitting in the shade reading a book, and Helen and Susan were sitting under an umbrella chatting. What caused my breath to catch and my blood pressure to rise was the sight of Zak and Isabella sitting at a patio table with their heads inches apart as they looked at something on the screen of Zak's laptop.

"You're back." Zak smiled at me when I walked over. "How was the Zoo?"

"It was fine. How was your morning?"

"Great."

"So what are you doing?" I asked.

Zak was sitting at the table, which was pushed up against the wall to his right, and Isabella was almost sitting on his lap to the left, so I was forced to sit down in a chair across from him.

"Zak is helping me work out the coding for a new game I'm developing," Isabella, who was wearing the tiniest bikini I had ever seen, said.

"You're working on another game together?" I asked.

"No, it's Isabella's game. I'm just helping her work through a couple of glitches she's been having," Zak, who was dressed in nothing but swim shorts, explained.

"I see." I tried to smile and look unaffected about the fact that Isabella was sitting so close to Zak that the hairs on his chest moved when she spoke.

"So what's on the agenda today?" I asked.

"The moms," Isabella nodded toward her mom and Zak's, "want to take you into town so they can help you choose a going-away outfit."

"A what?"

"The clothes you wear after the wedding. Mother Zimmerman is quite adamant that if you won't go on the trip she planned to give you for your honeymoon, you should allow her to buy your going-away outfit."

"And she wants to go shopping today?" I looked helplessly at Zak.

"It'll be fun," Zak encouraged. "I'll come with you to help you decide what to get."

"Oh, Zak, don't be silly." Isabella placed her hand on Zak's bare chest. "You can't go along. Buying a going-away outfit is a girl thing. I think it might be bad luck to see the bride's outfit before the wedding. I'm sure Zoe will be fine with the moms."

"I really just planned to wear jeans," I tried.

Isabella laughed. "Jeans. You've got yourself a funny one, Zak. Like anyone would wear jeans as a going-away outfit."

"But I'm not going anywhere," I argued. "I'm staying right here after the wedding. We aren't leaving for our trip until the next day."

Isabella shrugged. "It's up to you, but you'll never have any peace from Helen if you don't let her buy you something. And it will need to be something important. Something integral to the wedding."

I bit my lip. I suspected this whole thing was a ploy to get Zak alone, but I imagined she was right about the lack of peace from Helen if I didn't make some sort of a concession.

"You know," Zak began, "I think it might be a good idea if we took my mom to lunch and talked to her about her role in the wedding. Just Zoe and me."

"What about the kids?" I asked.

"I'm sure Isabella will watch them for a few hours."

"You want me to babysit?" Isabella turned red.

"It'll be fun. You can play video games with them. Scooter loves video games."

Zak got up from his seat and walked around the table. He lifted me into his arms and gave me a very intimate, very heartfelt kiss. The kiss seemed sort of random, considering we were in the midst of his family, but I suspected it was really for Isabella's benefit. If I didn't know better I'd say Zak was making a clear statement that would leave little doubt as to where his affections lay. I couldn't have loved him more.

I was dreading spending the afternoon with Zak's mom, but once we arrived at the restaurant it seemed like things were actually going okay. She seemed to have mellowed in the past couple of days. I still wouldn't want to be left alone with her for any length of time, but I could see that once we got this wedding behind us, we might have a foundation on which to build a relationship.

Maybe it was the glow of knowing that in a few short days I'd be Zak's wife, or maybe it was the two glasses of wine I'd had with lunch. Either way I found myself coming around to the idea that Mother Zimmerman and I could even be friends. We'd visit her, she'd visit us. I could see us cooking Thanksgiving dinner together or, more accurately, I could see us sipping wine and gossiping while Zak cooked dinner. I don't know what I'd been so worried about. She wasn't nearly as bad as I'd initially thought.

"I've put Baby Zimmerman on the wait list for Pemberton Academy," Mother Zimmerman announced.

I spit my wine across the table. "What?"

"Pemberton Academy is the best private school that money can buy. The wait list is ridiculously long. If you have any hope of getting your child in, you need to plan for these things."

"Zoe isn't pregnant, Mother."

"To be honest I wasn't certain." Mother Zimmerman looked me up and down. "It seems like she's thickened a bit."

"I haven't thickened," I defended myself, "and I'm not pregnant."

"Yes, well, if you aren't pregnant now I assume you will be soon. I really don't think we would be premature in signing up for the list. Trust me, when the time comes and little Zolton is ready to enter academia you will be glad I had the foresight to get him on the list."

Zolton?

"Mother, we aren't naming our son Zolton, should we have a son, and we aren't sending him to Pemberton Academy."

"What do you mean, you aren't sending him to Pemberton?" Mother Zimmerman snorted. "Whyever not?"

"For one thing, it's in Connecticut. We live in Ashton Falls."

Mother Zimmerman put down her fork. "Surely you don't plan to raise children in this hole in the wall? It is fine for a vacation spot, but it is nowhere to raise children."

"I was raised here," I pointed out.

"Yes, well . . ." Mother Zimmerman said that as if it were her point exactly.

"Zak went to school here from the seventh through the twelfth grade and he turned out fine," I added.

"Zachary is exceptional. Your children will be born into wealth. They can and should have every opportunity available to them. If you don't want to move to Connecticut Zolton can board."

"I'm not sending my children to boarding school," I almost screamed.

"Maybe we should talk about this later," Zak suggested.

I looked around the restaurant to find every eye on us.

"Yeah, maybe we should."

I ate the rest of my meal in silence. We all did. If the overbearing, meddling woman in front of me thought she was going to tell me how to raise my children she had another thing coming.

After we returned from town Charlie and I decided to go for a walk. I needed to clear my head and get away from all the Zimmerman DNA that had invaded my home. I started off with no specific destination in mind but ended up at the boathouse. The fact that I might not have Ellie to run to when things got rough, if Levi took the job he'd been offered and she decided to go with him, depressed me more than I wanted to deal with.

Ellie wasn't home, but I knew the Beach Hut didn't close for another couple of hours, so I sat on one of the chairs on her deck, or maybe it was my deck. I did still own the place. I wasn't sure what I expected from my wedding, but I was certain the level of stress I'd had to endure in the past month had been nowhere on my radar. I loved Zak and I wanted to be his wife, but I really hadn't anticipated what it meant to marry into his family. My family was great. They were loving and easygoing for the most part. But Zak's family . . . Could I really imagine having holidays with them every other year for the rest of my life?

"I thought I'd find you here." Zak sat down next to me.

"I'm sorry I left. I just needed to think."

"Don't worry about what my mom said. We're going to raise our children our way, and we aren't going to name our son Zolton. In fact, I say we make a pact right now and eliminate Z names from the list entirely."

"I couldn't agree more."

"I always thought if I had a son I'd name him Dynamo," Zak teased. "Dynamo Zimmerman. It has a ring to it."

I laughed. "I think we'd better leave baby names up to me."

"Yeah, maybe you're right." Zak took my hand, weaving his fingers through mine.

"Was she right?" I asked. "Do you have to get on a waiting list before your child is even a blip on the radar to get them into the best schools?"

"If we're talking Pemberton Academy, then probably yeah."

I leaned my head against Zak's shoulder. I remained silent as I watched a sailboat glide by in the distance. It was so calm and peaceful here and I couldn't imagine living anywhere else, but Zak's mom wasn't wrong. Our little underfunded school system wasn't going to provide the best education for our children, especially if our children had Zak's intelligence.

"Have you thought about it at all?" I asked. "Where we'll live and raise our children? Where they'll go to school?"

Zak laughed. "I sort of wanted to get a ring on your finger before I brought up something that controversial."

I smiled. "Smart man."

"But in answer to your question, yeah, I've thought about it. Indirectly. Last year, when I was looking for a school for Scooter, it occurred to me that one day I might be doing the same thing for our child."

"You thought about sending our child to boarding school?"

Zak hesitated. I could tell he realized that his answer was important. "It's not that I made any decisions about where our child might go to school. But I will say there's a part of me that wants the best of everything for any children we might have and, yeah, I guess that includes an excellent education."

I didn't respond.

"Some children do fine in an educational system such as the one Ashton Falls can offer. But other children—children like Alex—need a school that can meet their advanced rate of learning."

I thought about how lonely Alex was. How scared she was to take the next step in her academic future. I had to wonder if an advanced education was worth the cost of your childhood. I understood what Zak was saying, but I wanted the happy childhood I'd had for my children. I didn't want them to be sequestered away in some stringent learning environment. I wanted them to experience best-friend sleepovers, summer camping trips, hanging out after school, and Saturday matinees. I wanted them to have memories of the easier times of childhood that would see them through the often difficult times of adulthood.

"But we don't have to decide *now*," I emphasized. "We don't have to decide now."

Zak kissed the top of my head. "We absolutely do not have to decide now."

I returned my attention to the lake. It was so quiet and peaceful. I couldn't imagine living in a city, with the noise and pollution large metropolitan areas were apt to have. Of course the larger cities also offered cultural opportunities that we'd never have living in Ashton Falls. Still, if I had to pick, I'd choose to live in a small town that felt like a large family.

"You have a lot of money," I pointed out.

"I do."

"And when your new software comes out in the fall you'll have even more."

"We'll have even more," Zak agreed.

"You know, we could bring a superior education to us."

Zak paused. I turned to look at him. He seemed confused.

"You mean a private tutor?" he asked.

"I mean a private school. If Pemberton Academy is in Connecticut in a town no larger than this, why can't we bring the mountain to Muhammad and build our own private school right here?"

"You would want to do that?" Zak asked.

I thought of Alex. "If it would mean keeping those we love close by *and* providing them with a superior education. We could call it the Zimmerman Academy."

"You're serious about this."

"I guess I'm sort of serious. To be honest, the idea just popped into my head about thirty seconds ago, but building our own school would be a way for little Zolton, Zeus, Zena, Zelda, to have both an advanced education and a normal childhood."

Zak sat back in his chair. I knew he was considering my proposal. I hadn't told him about Alex. I hated to sway his opinion. Building a school—even a small one—wasn't something one did on a whim.

"I'm not talking about something huge. I think the school Scooter and Alex go to has about five hundred students," I assured him.

"Yeah, but Pemberton Academy has only two hundred," Zak pointed out. "And one of the schools I shopped when I was looking for a placement for Scooter had less than a hundred. I guess the school can be as large or as small as the person who establishes it wants it to be."

"I know this idea came out of nowhere and we would need to take everything into consideration, but I very much want our children to have a normal childhood. Did you know that Alex's parents are trying to get her accepted into a private high school next year?"

Zak frowned. "She told you that?"

"Yeah. And she's terrified. I remember thinking at the time that she'd be better off being homeschooled if she had outgrown her current school, but she pointed out that in order to be homeschooled you have to have a home."

"You're thinking of doing this school thing now?" Zak asked. "In time for Alex to attend?"

"Actually, the thought never entered my mind until this very minute, but wouldn't it be wonderful if she could stay with us? Scooter too."

Zak looked at me and laughed. "What happened to my child-phobic fiancée?"

I shrugged. "Beats me."

"Building a school would be a huge undertaking. And there's no way we could get it ready in time for Alex to attend next year. But I'm not against the idea of at least looking into it. It seems that it very well might be a good option for our own children. We could offer both a boarding and a day school option."

Zak tapped his fingertips against each other as he considered the idea. "Maybe we should talk to Phyllis."

"Because she was a college professor?" I asked.

"Because she not only grew up in a boarding school but was an administrator at a boarding school prior to deciding to teach at the university. I had a long talk with her when I was looking into schools for Scooter. She's very knowledgeable about the subject. Based on that conversation, I think we might be able to convince her to help us with this, should we decide to do it."

"Really?" Suddenly I was loving this idea. I really had no idea why. It wasn't like I didn't already have a million things on my plate. Of course Jeremy was already handling things at the Zoo, and once the wedding was over I wouldn't have that distraction.

"If you like the idea I think it's worth looking into," Zak said.

"But not in time for Alex."

"There's no way we can get permits, build a school, and hire staff in six weeks," Zak pointed out.

"Yeah, I guess you're right."

Zak laced his fingers through mine and gave my hand a squeeze. "Let me talk to Alex's parents to see what I can work out for her for this year."

"You would do that?"

"For you I would do anything."

Chapter 7

I decided to attend the regular Tuesday morning events committee meeting. I hadn't planned to. In fact, after last week's debacle, at which the committee had spent most of the meeting dissecting my wedding, I'd vowed not to. But somehow this morning I found a certain comfort in maintaining my normal routine.

I'd thought a lot about my discussion with Zak the previous evening. There were so many challenges ahead of us. So many huge decisions that would need to be made. I tried to remember a time in my life when rescuing animals and participating in community events was the only thing on my otherwise uncluttered mind.

"Zoe, I didn't expect to see you here this week." Hazel hugged me.

I was the first one to arrive and Hazel had come in next, so we were the only two in Rosie's back room.

"There's something to be said for following a routine in the midst of chaos."

"Yes, I guess I can see that. I heard you spoke to Newton Potter about using his barn for the Haunted Hamlet."

"I did. He's fine with it as long as we provide insurance and sign a maintenance contract. Levi and I took a drive out there to make sure it would meet our needs. I think it has real potential in spite of the ghosts."

"You think the place is actually haunted?" Hazel asked.

"If ghosts are real, then yeah, I think they're hanging out in Potter's barn. Do you know anything about the history of the place?" I asked as I poured myself a cup of coffee.

"No, not really. I do remember there was a death on the property some years ago. Other than that, nothing stands out as significant about it."

"After what happened at Hezekiah's place last year I'm thinking about doing a search before I commit. I wanted to have something in place before I left for my honeymoon, but I guess it will have to wait until I get back."

I added a doughnut to my plate and found a place to sit at the table.

Hazel poured her own cup of coffee and sat down next to me. "Let me see what I can find out. I'll search online as well as the newspaper archives at the library."

"Thanks. I'd appreciate that."

"I wanted to thank you again for letting Phyllis and me intrude on your day with Alex the other day. We do find we miss the girl when she's gone."

"Yeah. She really grows on you," I agreed. "Phyllis called to ask if she could have Alex over today so they could work on her story. It's too bad Alex can't make friends her own age as easily as she does with the adults in her life."

"Alex has trouble making friends?" Hazel asked. I could see the look of concern on her face and explained about the challenges she faced being so much smarter than her peers.

Hazel nodded. "Yes, I can see how that would be difficult."

"I just feel so bad for her." I picked off an end of my doughnut and popped it into my mouth. "In my mind sending her to high school would be a horrible idea even if her parents managed to get the waiver they're after. She's just a kid. An incredibly smart and mature kid, but a kid nonetheless. Zak is going to talk to them to see if he can work out an alternative."

"If there's anything I can do, be sure to let me know. I know Phyllis would help out as well. Even Ethan talks nonstop about the girl."

"I didn't know Ethan and Alex knew each other." Ethan Carlton was a retired history professor.

"Alex was doing a history project last semester and she mentioned to Phyllis that she was having a hard time finding reference material for one portion of it. Phyllis put her in touch with Ethan. I guess the two of them hit it off and have been e-mailing each other ever since. I wouldn't be at all surprised if he isn't at Phyllis's at this very moment. She's really very good with adults. It's a shame she can't make friends her own age."

The arrival of Willa, along with Tawny, put an end to our discussion, but I could see Hazel was as bothered by Alex's situation as I was.

"Zoe, what are you doing here?" Willa asked as she sat down across from Hazel and me.

"I wasn't busy, so I figured I'd attend." I decided to keep my answer simple.

"I heard about Pack Rat. I'm guessing you're investigating?"

Why did everyone assume I was investigating?

"Not officially," I answered. "I heard Pack Rat saw you arguing with a man with a small head."

Willa laughed. "That would be the janitor the county just hired. I've never met a man so bad at his job. I think the place is actually dirtier after he's been there. The last time he was in, not only did he not vacuum but he cut across the wet grass rather than taking the sidewalk and tracked a load of mud into my reception area."

"It sounded like the whole small-head thing was what creeped Pack Rat out."

"I remember seeing him that day. He started to come over to talk to me, but then he turned around and walked away. I wondered why he took off."

"It's so odd to think that he's gone from our lives," Tawny added. "Not that I really knew him, but he was such a regular fixture in the alley behind the shops on Main. It's going to seem strange not to see him making his rounds. I think the merchants are going to miss him."

"Not everyone," Willa said. "I'd received several complaints in the last week or so from the project manager at the construction site at the new strip mall. I hate to say it, but if Pack Rat hadn't died he might have ended up in jail. I tried to convince him to stay away from the construction site, but he was like a dog with a bone. He absolutely refused to do as I requested."

"Did he say why he was so fixated on that particular site?" I asked.

"No, he didn't say, but the real problems didn't occur until after he started hanging around with that friend of his. I'd imagine this Stubby was behind the whole thing."

Gilda, Levi, and my dad, Hank Donovan, wandered in and took seats at the table while Willa was speaking.

"That Stubby character is bad news," my dad confirmed. "Prior to his arrival, Pack Rat would simply 'rescue' the odds and ends the merchants would toss into the Dumpsters, but I'm pretty sure Stubby actually broke into Trish's place."

Trish Carson owned Trish's Treasures, one of the six shops that made up the old town block that shared a building, including Bears and Beavers and Outback Hunting and Fishing.

"What was taken?" I asked.

"Just some random stuff, nothing of value. Trish told me the total haul couldn't have amounted to more than twenty dollars. But the really strange thing was, two days after the break-in Trish found a twenty-dollar bill sitting on her countertop near the cash register. She has no idea where it came from, but she suspected the thief was trying to pay her back."

"Why would anyone go to all the effort of breaking in to a place, take only penny items, and then leave the money to pay for it a few days later?" Hazel asked.

"The whole thing makes no sense," I agreed. "Why do you suspect Stubby?"

"He has a look about him, and the break-ins didn't occur prior to his showing up in town," my dad said.

"Do you know when Trish's place was vandalized?" I asked.

My dad thought about it. "We talked about it when we ran into each other at the Beach Hut on Wednesday of last week. She mentioned it happened the previous Wednesday."

"The whole thing seems so random," Tawny commented.

"I spoke to Horton over at Outback Hunting and Fishing after I spoke to you yesterday," Gilda informed me. "He also said it was his belief that he had missing inventory. He was going to go back to recheck his records. When I mentioned to him that I had seen Stubby lurking around behind his store he was even more convinced that a theft had occurred."

"Did someone leave cash on his counter?" I asked.

"Not as far as I know."

"Sounds like Salinger needs to round this Stubby up and have a chat with him," Levi suggested.

"I couldn't agree more. I'm going to step outside to call him. Please go ahead and start the meeting without me if everyone is here," I said.

After I called Salinger, who did promise to look into the theft angle, I returned to the meeting, where the upcoming Haunted Hamlet was being discussed. I was both overwhelmed at being chair and excited by the awesome ideas everyone was coming up with. I had the feeling this was going to be the best Haunted Hamlet the town of Ashton Falls had ever seen.

"Last year most of the food vendors set up in the park," Tawny offered. "While I can see the wisdom in having the food where there are plenty of tables to eat at, I think it would be nice to have smaller vendors placed around town, like we do for Christmas Carnival."

"If people can buy food along Main Street they're more apt to bring their food and drinks into nearby stores," Gilda said. "The last thing I need is caramel from caramel apples all over my inventory."

I tried to feign interest in the conversation, but I had much more serious things on my mind than sticky fingers and spilled beverages. I sat quietly, trying to at least look like I was paying attention until Willa finally called the meeting to an end and we were free to go our separate ways.

I headed over to Second Hand Suzie's, which was just down the alley from Rosie's. Gilda had indicated that Suzie's store was one of those that had fallen victim to random thefts, and I was curious to find out what had been taken. I was beginning to see a pattern, though it made no sense, and I generally like things to make sense.

"Morning, Suzie," I greeted her.

"Zoe." Suzie gave me a hug. "I'm so glad you stopped by. I wanted to have a chance to wish you luck on Saturday."

"Are you coming to the wedding?"

"I'm afraid it's my sister's birthday and I already promised to spend the day with her. We're going shopping in Bryton Lake, but I'll be with you in spirit."

"Thank you; I appreciate that. I guess you heard about Pack Rat."

A wave of grief crossed Suzie's face. "I did. I really miss him stopping by to rescue my discarded items and share a story."

"When was the last time you saw him?" I asked.

"On Thursday. It wasn't our best visit. He seemed distracted. Like something lay heavy on his mind. I was hoping he'd finish his tale about the Dollinger gang, but he said he didn't feel up to a story."

"The Dollinger gang?"

"They were bandits from a long time ago. I guess they lived in town when Ashton Falls was still Devil's Den. Pack Rat had started to tell me the story about the brothers robbing a stagecoach that was carrying cash from the local bank to a larger one in the city when he realized he needed to go for some reason."

"Was Stubby with him?"

"No, Pack Rat was alone. I sort of hoped Stubby had moved on and asked Pack Rat about him, but he said his friend was just 'otherwise detained.'"

"Gilda mentioned you were burglarized a while back."

"Yes," Suzie confirmed. "It was a couple of weeks ago. Nothing of value was taken. I most likely wouldn't even have noticed it, but the lock on the back door was damaged, so I looked around."

"After the break-in did you happen to find money just lying around?" I asked.

Suzie looked surprised. "Why, yes. I found forty dollars tucked into the basket of scarves I keep on the counter a couple of days later."

"And was the value of the missing items around forty dollars?"

Suzie thought about it. "Yes, I guess that would be about right. Do you think someone had second thoughts and decided to pay restitution?"

"Perhaps. What doesn't add up is that you were robbed a couple of weeks ago. Gilda was vandalized just a few days ago. If the burglar felt remorse why did he strike again?"

"Good question. I tend to have more than my fair share of senior moments. I suppose it's possible I tucked the forty dollars into the basket without even realizing it. I found a pair of earrings I would have sworn I hung on the rack in the cash register last week."

After speaking to Suzie I headed back over to the market to speak to Ernie. Gilda was correct in the fact that he knew Pack Rat better than most. While he visited many of the vendors along Main Street and even stopped to chat with most, he seemed to have developed an actual friendship with Ernie.

The market Ernie owned and operated was the only grocery store in Ashton Falls. He made a point of speaking to his customers, and because everyone has to eat, Ernie pretty much knew everyone who lived in Ashton Falls.

"I was just going to call you," Ernie said when I walked into the front door of the market.

"Really? Why?"

"My clerk told me that you were in here looking for me yesterday."

"Yeah, I wanted to talk to you about Pack Rat. Do you have a minute?"

"Let's go back to my office."

Ernie motioned to his clerk to watch the front counter while we were in the back.

"I'm glad to see you're investigating," Ernie began as he motioned for me to take a seat across from his desk. "Pack Rat was a little rough around the edges, but he was a good guy, and he didn't deserve to die that way."

"Do you have any idea who might have wanted to hurt him?" I asked.

"Perhaps." Ernie adjusted his position so that he was looking directly at me. "I've thought about this a lot since I learned Pack Rat was murdered. On one hand, it seemed like everyone got along with the guy, but it did seem like something was off the past few weeks."

"Stubby?"

"Maybe. If I had to guess, I'd say Pack Rat knew Stubby from his past. I don't know how exactly, but the first time Pack Rat introduced me to the guy I could tell that the dynamic between them was off. I don't think Pack Rat liked the guy, but he either felt he owed him a debt of some sort or he was afraid of something the man knew."

Ernie was the third person to mention that the relationship between Pack Rat and Stubby was off. I was certain this had to be an important clue.

"Do you think Pack Rat was being blackmailed by Stubby?" I asked.

"I don't know. Maybe. Prior to the introduction of Stubby to the mix, Pack Rat has always been a loner. It doesn't make sense that all of a sudden he'd be going around town introducing this man if they'd only just met. And like I said, the dynamic seemed off."

"Salinger told me earlier that he's been looking for Stubby ever since I found Pack Rat's body. Do you happen to know where he was staying or where he might be now?"

"I don't know for certain, although I guess I just assumed he was staying at the cabin. I haven't seen him since Pack Rat's body was found, so maybe he took off."

I was certain one of the first places Salinger would have looked for Stubby was at Pack Rat's cabin, so chances were he was no longer there, if he had ever been there in the first place. Still, it wouldn't hurt to head over there when I was done in the market to check it out.

"Do you know anything at all about Pack Rat's past?" I asked. "Anything that could lead us to a clue to what might have happened to him?"

Ernie paused. He seemed to be considering my question.

"We found an empty bottle of whiskey on the seat next to Pack Rat," I informed him. "As far as you know, did he have a drinking problem?"

"He did at one point," Ernie admitted. "But he's been sober for years. I think that once he dealt with the trauma of his past he found a certain inner peace in the life he chose."

"Trauma?"

"Pack Rat was a prisoner of war during the military action in Vietnam."

I couldn't imagine being locked up by people who didn't even speak the same language as you, not knowing from one day to the next whether you were going to live or die.

"I didn't realize he was that old."

"He enlisted in 1972, when he was eighteen. He was assigned to a combat unit right off the bat. Pack Rat didn't like to talk about his past. I got the sense that it was so horrible that he couldn't live with the memory of what had happened to him. When he first got back to the United States he drowned himself in a bottle, but at some point he realized he didn't want to live his life as a drunk, so he quit drinking and moved to Ashton Falls. He said he found he could breathe up here on the mountain, away from noise and people."

"Wow. I had no idea."

"He had a little money saved up, which he used to buy the cabin he lived in. He told me that every time he'd get the urge to drink he'd distract himself with treasure hunting. I know that from the outside looking in, living the life he did was pathetic at best, but he really seemed to enjoy being free from the constraints of having a job or money, or any responsibility, really. He was a pleasant sort and those he knew gave him food and money. He seemed to do okay."

"Do you think Stubby was in some way associated with his past?" I asked.

"I don't know for certain, but I'd guess he was. The two men seem to be about the same age. I don't know if Pack Rat knew Stubby from his time in the army or his time on the street as a drunk, but I definitely picked up on the vibe that there was a history between the two men."

"I don't suppose you happen to know Pack Rat's real name?" I asked.

"Sorry. He never said."

I thanked Ernie and turned to leave. I was certain Salinger would want to know about the military connection.

"Oh," I added, before I exited Ernie's office, "I've had a couple of people tell me that they believe Stubby was stealing from the merchants Pack Rat introduced him to. Do you know if you're missing anything?"

"Not as far as I know."

"Pack Rat borrowed the truck he was found in. Do you have any idea why he might have done that?"

"Not a clue."

I decided to head over to Pack Rat's cabin after I left the market. I doubted there was much to find there, but it couldn't hurt to look.

When you pulled onto the dirt road that led to Pack Rat's home you immediately noticed the trail of "artifacts" lining both sides of the drive. By the time you arrived at the cabin the yard was so cluttered as to find no ground uncovered. I'd been inside Pack Rat's home in the past and knew from experience that the place was so full as to be impenetrable. I wasn't sure if the door would be unlocked, but I climbed the front steps and tried the knob anyway. I have to admit I was somewhat surprised to find the door wide open. Pack Rat had a lot of stuff and none of it appeared to be worth anything, but he did seem to be protective of his treasures.

The problem with trying to find clues among the mess was the sheer mass of the items contained within Pack Rat's domain. There could be a big fat clue sitting in plain sight, but the likelihood of my picking it out in the clutter was slim to none.

The one thing my eye did gravitate toward was a food bowl on the porch near the door. It looked like Pack Rat had been feeding an animal. Most likely a stray cat. I decided to concentrate my efforts there because a cat, at least, was something I knew how to identify and deal with.

"Here, kitty, kitty," I called.

I didn't see or hear anything at first, but after several minutes I heard the most pathetic meow.

I looked out across the debris field and tried to figure out where the sound was coming from. The cat could be anywhere. I began to walk toward the center of the yard, being careful not to trip over anything as I made my way toward the place I'd thought I'd heard the cat.

"I'm not going to hurt you," I cooed. "I just want to feed you."

Nothing.

I looked around some more, continuing to call the cat, but it hadn't made a sound since the first meow. I supposed my wandering around could be making it nervous. It occurred to me that maybe I should put some food in the bowl. That might lure the feline out of hiding. I headed back toward the cabin and prayed I wouldn't get lost forever among Pack Rat's possessions as I searched for some cat food.

I stood in the doorway to the cabin and looked in at the sea of treasures. Did Pack Rat even have a kitchen? I certainly didn't see one. I was about to turn around and figure out another plan when I noticed something out of the corner of my eye. I was about to investigate further when I felt a furry feline rubbing against my leg.

I bent over and picked her up. "You ready to get out of here?"

"Meow."

"Yeah, me too."

Chapter 8

Later that evening I sat on the deck of the boathouse and watched a beach full of dogs playing as I shared a meal with my closest friends. I hadn't wanted a party, but I had to admit that this particular party had turned out just right. It was a warm evening without so much as a breeze to mar the perfection of the lake.

"So did the cat I brought by settle in okay?" I asked Tiffany.

"She did. It was a good thing you thought to go out to the cabin. The poor dear was starving. My sense is that Pack Rat has been feeding her since she was a kitten. I'm sure there are plenty of mice running around Pack Rat's property, but she doesn't appear to have had the sense to catch and eat them."

"I'd like to find her an awesome home. I have a feeling she's lived as an outdoor cat to this point, but it seems she really likes people, so I'm sure she can adjust to any situation."

"I had Scott stop by on his way home today," Tiffany said, referring to the local veterinarian who also volunteered at the Zoo.

"He said she has some intestinal parasites we'll need to deal with before adopting her out. He has her on medication, so she should be fine in a week or so. I'll start a list of good prospects from the names we have on file as prospective adoptive parents. Maybe an older woman with a comfy lap?"

"Comfy laps are the best," I agreed.

"Did you find anything else interesting while you were there?" Jessica Anderson, Jeremy's girlfriend, asked. "I've always wanted to sort through that place. I bet there are really valuable items mixed in with the trash."

"There were a lot of interesting items. Too many. It would take a year to sort through all of Pack Rat's treasures and I really didn't have time. I did notice that there was some nice furniture inside. Some might be actual antiques."

"I wonder who'll have to sort through all of that now that Pack Rat is deceased," Ellie's assistant, Kelly Arlington, said.

"Good question," I acknowledged. "So far we don't even know who he really is. Even if Salinger figures that out I doubt there are next of kin just waiting for their inheritance."

"Everyone belongs to someone," Kelly murmured.

She had a point. Based on what Ernie had told me, Pack Rat wasn't close to his family, but that didn't mean he didn't have one. It would be interesting to see if whoever ended up with Pack Rat's treasures cared about them at all.

"My grandfather was a bit of a pack rat," Jessica shared. "Nothing like our Pack Rat, but he had this detached garage that was filled front to back and top to bottom with things he picked up at garage sales. He used to tell everyone that he was going to make a bunch of money off his finds one day at a flea market, but he never bothered to make an effort to sell any of the stuff. Anyway, the family was pretty much convinced it was just a bunch of trash, but after he died and we cleaned out that old garage we found a lot of pretty valuable stuff."

"I suppose it would be fun to go through Pack Rat's cabin," Kelly responded. "It would be like a treasure hunt."

"I can't help but think that Pack Rat's treasure hunting might have gotten him killed," I commented. "Willa told me that she'd had some complaints, including a pretty harsh one from the developer of the new strip mall."

"City folks don't understand our country ways," one of my old friends from school added. "I don't know why our town council agreed to let that eyesore be built anyway."

"Oh, I don't know," Jessica responded. "I heard the new mall is going to have a Ferguson's Shoes. At first I really didn't support the idea of a strip mall in our town either, but to be that close to that many shoes without having to drive for an hour? Heaven."

"Have you heard what other shops are going in?" Ellie asked. She had just joined us from the kitchen, where she had been mixing up another pitcher of drinks.

"I know there's going to be a hardware store and a medical supply store," Jessica answered. "Neither of which are as exciting as a shoe store."

"I heard there's going to be a discount florist," I offered. "I think Pam is pretty concerned about her business, and I don't blame her."

"Having a little competition between vendors might work out well for the community as a whole," Tawny said. "It's a lot less expensive to shop in Bryton Lake, but then, Bryton Lake has multiple proprietors selling the same products, so they compete for business."

"I doubt you'd be saying that if there was going to be a new day care center in the mall," Ellie added.

Tawny shrugged. "I suppose that's true. Still, I hope the mall brings in some clothing stores."

"When I was in the mall in Bryton Lake last week one of the salesclerks told me we're getting a Forever Fantastic," Kelly shared.

Forever Fantastic was a popular clothing store that really would be a huge asset to our somewhat isolated community, although I'm sure proprietors of shops like Country Cousins and Mountain Sportswear were less than thrilled with that particular addition.

"I love that store." Tawny beamed.

"Is your dad worried about the hardware store that's going in?" Tiffany asked me.

"He says he isn't. He'll be fine financially even if Donovan's doesn't survive the competition, but the store means a lot to him. It will break his heart to lose it."

"I wonder if they're going to put in any new restaurants," Jessica mused.

"If there aren't at this point I'm sure one will show up eventually," Kelly said with confidence. "I know when the small town I grew up in got its first mall everyone thought the threat to existing businesses would be limited to the shops, but the mall brought in so much traffic that supporting retailers like restaurants, gas stations, even other stores, grew up around it. In the end the business center of our town shifted completely."

"Yeah, but the mall isn't on the lake," Ellie argued. "I doubt visitors, especially, will favor the shops in the mall over those that are already along Main Street."

Kelly shrugged. "Perhaps. Still, I won't be surprised to see a shift of some sort, even if it isn't abrupt."

"Did you ever find out what Pack Rat was so excited about finding in the trash at the construction site?" Ellie asked me.

"No. It did occur to me that the information might be important, but there was nothing in the truck when I found him, and his place is such a mess that I had no way of knowing what's new and what's been there for years. Unless we stumble across some new evidence or an eyewitness, I'm not sure the object of his desire will ever be identified."

"You know, when Pack Rat stopped by the Hut on Friday he mentioned selling something he'd found," Kelly offered.

"Really? Pack Rat never seemed to sell anything," I commented. "You've seen his place."

"I don't disagree, but in this case he definitely had selling on his mind," Kelly verified. "He mentioned several times that he had prospective buyers to meet."

"Did he say what he planned to sell?" I asked.

"No. But I got the impression it was something valuable."

"I wonder what he wanted the money for," Tiffany said.

"He didn't tell me." Kelly shrugged. "I sort of got the feeling he wanted the money for something specific, though. To be honest, I was busy; Ellie was off rescuing Zoe, and I was only half-listening to the guy as he rambled on. If I knew what was going to happen I would have paid a lot closer attention."

"Plus you'd just gotten back to work after being sick," Jessica pointed out. "I'm sure you weren't a hundred percent."

Kelly looked directly at me, begging me with her eyes not to say anything about the fact that I knew she hadn't actually been sick. The makeup I'd recommended was as terrific as everyone said it was. You couldn't tell that her lowlife boyfriend had beaten her up.

"Did Jason ever look into a job opening at the construction site?" I asked Kelly. When I'd been by her place the previous week she'd mentioned that her boyfriend was stressed over losing his job, which she'd offered as the reason behind his brutal attack.

"I told him about it, but I'm not sure whether he's had a chance to follow up."

"My next-door neighbor got a job doing framing," Jessica told her. "They're offering union wages. It's a good gig. You should definitely persuade Jason to check it out."

"Yeah, I will."

"You know, this is really nice," Tiffany said, looking around. "We should do this more often. It's nice to have a girls' night out every now and then."

"Zoe is about to get married. I'm betting girls' nights are going to be off the table for her," Kelly commented.

"Hey, I can still do girls' nights," I defended myself.

"And Ellie is all but engaged," Jessica added. "Bet it won't be long now."

I watched Ellie as her face fell.

"So, did someone mention presents?" I quickly changed the subject before Ellie burst into tears.

"Just wait until you see what I got for you." Tiffany grinned. "Zak is going to love it."

"See, that wasn't so bad," Ellie said after the others had left and it was just the two of us.

"Actually, it was really fun. I'm glad you bullied me into doing it."

"That's what best friends are for.'

"When you get married and it's my turn to play maid of honor, I promise to throw you an equally awesome bachelorette party."

Ellie sighed. "At this point I'm operating under the assumption I'm never getting married."

"Of course you will. I know you feel like you've hit a bump in the road, but if there was ever anyone meant for the whole marriage-kids-picket fence-minivan thing, it's you."

"I used to think that, but with everything that's happened lately, I'm not so sure. First my fiancé leaves me for his ex. Then I find out I'm probably never going to be able to have children of my own. Then something wonderful happens and I finally get together with Levi. But now . . . now he's probably leaving and I'll never see him again."

"Of course you'll see him again. Even if he takes the job he's not moving that far away. You'll see him all the time."

"Maybe. But it won't be the same. *We* won't be the same."

I didn't say anything because Ellie was right. It *wouldn't* be the same.

"Has he definitely decided to go?" I asked.

"He's conditionally decided to go. He still wants to meet with the head coach to talk through the specifics of his duties and responsibilities before he gives notice at Ashton Falls High. I guess the coach is out of the country and won't be back for a couple of weeks, but I know he plans to make the trip to speak to him as soon as he gets back. If Levi takes the job he'll have to leave Ashton Falls almost immediately."

"Oh, El. I'm so sorry." I leaned over and gave her a best-friend hug. The long, hard kind that only best friends can give.

"Things have been going so well," Ellie cried. "I really thought we had a chance."

"And you're sure you don't want to go with him?" I asked.

"He still hasn't exactly asked. He's working under the assumption that we'll do the long-distance thing until he sees how the job works out. After that? Who knows?"

"If he did ask you to go, would you?"

"I'm not sure. I have my business here. And I love living in the boathouse. My mom and all of my friends are here. You're here. If Levi takes the job he'll be busy and I'll be left to make new friends and build a new life on my own. I really don't think I'm up for that." Ellie turned and looked directly at me. "If Zak was offered a job in another town would you go?"

"In a heartbeat."

"Yeah. That's what I figured. Sometimes I wonder if I love Levi as much as I think I do."

I frowned. "What do you mean?"

"It's like this: At first we were friends. Best friends, along with you. And for twenty years that was fine. It was better than fine; it was perfect. But then I started having feelings for him that definitely were not of the best-friend variety. I thought about him all the time, and I was certain we could live happily ever after, but I wanted children and he didn't, so we never acted on those feelings. He moved in with Barbie, I got engaged to Rob. We both chose, at least temporarily, to allow this one huge difference in perspective to make a difference in our relationship. It was only after the conflict was removed, after I found out I couldn't have children, that we allowed ourselves to give in to the lusty feelings we'd been having for each other for months."

Ellie paused to take a breath. I waited for her to continue.

"Now another conflict has arisen, and it seems like we're back to square one. If our relationship is real shouldn't it be able to handle a conflict? You just said that you would follow Zak wherever life might take him. I know you love Ashton Falls as much as I do, but you didn't even hesitate. It seems to me that your level of commitment is the way a real relationship should be."

I had to admit Ellie wasn't wrong. I knew she and Levi cared for each other, but I also knew that if their love was as solid as the one Zak and I shared it should be able to withstand the challenges it was bound to face along the way. Zak and I had certainly survived in spite of challenges.

"So what are you saying?" I asked.

Ellie let out a slow breath. "I don't know. I don't want to overreact and destroy what Levi and I have over this one conflict, but I'd be lying if I didn't say it's causing me to take an honest look at the level of our commitment. I love Levi. He's very important to me. But I know that if we act in haste we'll destroy not only the romantic relationship we've developed but our friendship as well. I really think we need to take some time to ask ourselves why it is that we both seem to be so unwilling to sacrifice for each other. If he goes to State, even if he asks me to go with him, I'm pretty sure I've made up my mind I'm not going too. At least not until I'm sure I can answer the question about my willingness to go with as much certainty as you just did."

I reached over and hugged Ellie. I knew she had to be in so much pain. I hoped things would work out for her and Levi. They did seem to make a perfect couple, but her concerns seemed legitimate.

"Is there anything I can do?" I asked.

Ellie smiled a weak, sad little smile. "No. Not really. I guess Levi and I just need to work through this. I do know that the friendship I share with him is the most important thing to me. I'd rather break up with him now and remain friends than continue in a relationship with an expiration date clearly in view. I'm afraid that if we force something that doesn't come naturally we'll end up hating each other. I may not be certain of much, but I am certain I can't live with that."

"Do you think you *can* go back to being just friends?" I wondered.

"I have no idea. I'd like to think we could, but maybe, after everything I've just said, it's already much too late. I know it would kill me to see him with another woman."

A single tear slid down Ellie's cheek. "If we do decide to return to friends-only status I'm going to have to learn how to control my jealous side."

"That," I assured my best friend, "is something I've had a lot of practice doing. It isn't easy to rein in an emotion as strong as jealousy, but I've found that with practice it's possible. I didn't say easy, and I have a ways to go myself, but I made a decision a while back to try to be the woman Zak already seems to think I am. I don't know if you and Levi are meant to be together as a romantically committed couple, but I do know you love each other, and it would destroy you both if you let anything happen to your friendship. As much as it may suck to do so, sometimes all you can do is let the situation play out."

Ellie put her arms around me, burying her face in my neck as she wept. I hugged her as tightly as I could and wept with her. One of the hardest things there is to endure in life is to see someone you care about in pain, when you know you're unable to do anything to alleviate that pain. I loved both Levi and Ellie, and in my heart I had to believe that someday they'd have their happily ever after.

Chapter 9

I woke up to find that not only had Cousin Twyla and her disruptive spawn come to town a whole day early but Eric's grandmother was on the premises as well.

"Tell me again why Eric's grandmother can't stay with the others in the house my mom rented," I asked Zak as he sat on the bed beside me wearing nothing but his best I'm-sorry expression.

God, he's adorable.

"Because Nona and my mom don't get along at all. One of them will have to stay here, and Mom is already settled at the guesthouse, so I figured it made sense for Nona to stay here. Besides, Nona doesn't care for Twyla's children, and we certainly don't want *them* staying with us."

I frowned as I tried to make sense of all the Zimmerman relations. "So Eric is your cousin but Nona isn't your grandmother?"

"Eric is the only child of my mom's younger sister, Wanda, and her first husband, Theodore. Nona is Theodore's mother, so she isn't actually related to me, although she's considered family."

"Okay, so it was Nona's husband who came up with the crazy will that required Eric and Cindy to be married for five years before he could collect the bulk of his inheritance? He's obviously dead. How about Theodore? Is he still among the living?"

"No, he passed away when Eric was a child. It's been Eric's mother and Nona who have ruled over him for pretty much his entire life."

"No wonder he has no idea how to have a healthy relationship with a woman. So Nona is in Ashton Falls in spite of the fact that she doesn't get along with your mother, but Wanda, who also doesn't get along with your mother, isn't planning to attend."

"As far as I know."

"And Nona has an opinion about Twyla's children, although she isn't related to them either?"

"Correct. Twyla is Darlene's sister. They both belong to my mother's youngest brother, Joseph."

I was definitely getting a headache. "You know, I just realized that if Darlene is your mother's niece her last name shouldn't be Zimmerman. Isn't Zimmerman your father's surname?"

"No. My biological father's surname is Connolly. My mother kept her maiden name when she married, and when I was born she gave that name to me."

"You certainly do have some strong women in your family."

Zak grinned. "Tell me about it."

I smiled. "Don't you think it's odd that we're sitting here stark naked talking about your family?"

"I think it's odd that we're wasting time talking about my family at all." Zak pulled me into his arms.

"You started it by bringing up Nona," I reminded him as he kissed my neck.

"And now I'm changing the subject." He trailed his kisses lower.

By the time we joined the others it was well into midmorning. Everyone knew we'd attended our bachelor and bachelorette parties the previous evening, so it was assumed we were simply hung over. Which we weren't, but it was a convenient excuse to sleep in, and we went with it.

"How's the headache?" Darlene asked.

"It's fine now," I answered. "It looks like the gang is all here." I looked out toward the pool area, which was covered with tanned bodies.

"Not everyone is here, but there are quite a few of us who have migrated over. The pool here is a lot better than the one in the rental, so Twyla and I decided to come and crash yours. When everyone found out what we were doing the others tagged along. To be honest, I think the only reason Aunt Helen didn't come is because she wanted to have a break from Twyla's kids."

"Are they really that bad?"

Darlene nodded. "Yes, they really are. But don't worry; the demon spawn haven't broken anything yet."

"I realize you believe your niece and nephew to be a handful, but don't you think referring to them as demon spawn is a bit over the top? They are, after all, children."

"Just wait until you meet them."

I took a deep breath. "I guess there's no time like the present. Is Nona here too?"

"She's resting in her room. I guess she traveled all night to get here. Have you met her yet?"

"No. Not yet."

Darlene grinned.

"Is she really that bad?"

"It's not that, exactly. I really like her. Let's just say she's an acquired taste that a lot of family members simply can't deal with. She has a very strong personality and doesn't take the opinions of others into consideration at all. Aunt Helen absolutely can't tolerate her. In fact, I'm pretty sure Nona only came to the wedding because she knew it would stick in her craw, and if there's one thing Nona loves, it's messing with Aunt Helen."

Great. Just what I needed, an opinionated matriarch who got some sort of perverted joy out of annoying people.

"I guess I'll just have to keep an open mind," I decided. "For now, why don't you introduce me to Twyla and her children?"

After Darlene's assessment of the situation I was expecting to be greeted with total mayhem, but things seemed to be mostly under control. Darlene introduced me to Twyla's children, who were playing nicely in the pool with Scooter, Alex, and Tucker. She then introduced me to Twyla, who was sitting with Eric and Jimmy, pounding down beer after beer even though it was a good two hours until lunch. No one was arguing and I didn't see any signs of bloodshed. Satisfied that all was well with the world, I decided to take Charlie and Bella and go for a run.

The first thing I noticed when leaving the house was a pink Harley. I turned around and reentered the building I'd just vacated.

"Do you know that there's a Harley in our front drive?" I asked Zak. "A pink Harley, to be more specific."

"It belongs to Nona."

"Nona?"

I have to admit that when Zak had spoken about the woman I'd pictured a shriveled-up old prune with vinegar for blood and a sourpuss attitude. At times I'd even imagined her as tall, with talons to destroy her prey, or as withered and stooped with age. But in all my fantasies I hadn't seen her wearing the pink leather jacket tossed carelessly across the sofa. When I'd seen it there earlier I'd just assumed it belonged to Twyla, or maybe Darlene.

"It's her pride and joy," Zak confirmed.

"The woman who has a reputation for ruling with an iron fist rides a Harley?"

I supposed in a way it made sense. But still . . .

"Nona is not only a strong and opinionated woman but she's just a tiny bit crazy. And I don't mean crazy as in fun-loving and spontaneous. I mean straight-up, howl-at-the-moon crazy."

I smiled. "I really can't wait to meet her."

"And you shall. As soon as she rests up from her trip."

I turned to leave. I glanced over my shoulder. "Howl at the moon?"

Zak shrugged.

I thought I was going to love this woman.

I didn't intend to work on my investigation into Pack Rat's death when I set out, but I couldn't get Kelly's statement about Pack Rat's intention to sell something out of my mind. Could the sale have gone badly and resulted in his death? As far as I knew, it was out of character for Pack Rat to sell any of his treasures, so if he planned to do so now it must have been for a very good reason. Of course, I realized that figuring out what that reason was would be pretty much impossible now that the man was dead.

Whatever happened, it had been on Friday. Pack Rat was driving his borrowed, beat-up old pickup on Friday. The vehicle was an eyesore. Chances were that there were people who'd noticed him around town. Maybe I could stitch together a timeline of his movements in an attempt to identify where he might have gotten into trouble.

Of course Pack Rat's murder might not have anything to do with his actions on Friday and I would be wasting my time. Maybe I really should just let Salinger deal with things this time around. Pretty much everyone I'd talked to lately had reminded me that I had a wedding to prepare for.

But, being completely honest with myself, I really did welcome an excuse to get away from the house, and a little investigation couldn't hurt.

"Geez, now I'm arguing with myself," I said to the dogs as we turned away from the beach into town.

Neither dog answered, but I was sure they agreed.

"A mature and responsible hostess would be at home hostessing," I added.

Charlie barked his agreement.

"It's only an irresponsible and selfish woman who would be actively looking for a reason to shirk her responsibilities."

Charlie pretty much ignored me.

"I guess we should go back," I said with dread in my voice.

Charlie looked up at me.

I was about to turn around and face the relatives when my phone rang. It was Salinger.

Oh, thank God.

"Salinger," I answered, feeling grateful that he had given me a reason to delay my return to the insanity awaiting me at the house.

"Donovan. Am I going to have to start referring to you as Zimmerman after Saturday?"

"Donovan is fine. What's up?"

"James Baldwin."

"James Baldwin?" I asked. In spite of the abrupt introduction it appeared I was in for a long conversation, so I walked over to a grassy spot in the shade so the dogs could rest.

"James Baldwin is Pack Rat Nelson's real name."

"Really?" I crossed my legs and plopped down on the ground next to the dogs. "I figured his last name really was Nelson at least."

"Not according to the military records I managed to track down. James enlisted in 1972. In 1974 he was listed as a POW. He was released in 1975. He had a string of petty crimes that all appear to be alcohol-related spanning the years 1975 to 1995. In 1995 he moved to Ashton Falls."

"If he was in the military why didn't his fingerprints show up the first time you checked?" I wondered.

"They've been altered. We got the ID from DNA. It took a while to get the results."

"Does he have any family?" I asked as I waved to a group of high school students who were, I guessed, heading to the beach.

"His oldest brother John passed away shortly before James enlisted. His next oldest brother Patrick enlisted at the same time. He was killed in the war. The parents are deceased, but he does have a number of aunts and uncles."

"Okay, while this is interesting, does it help us?" I asked as I reached the arm that wasn't attached to the hand holding the phone over my head in order to stretch out my back.

"It fills in some of the blanks, but no, I'm not sure it brings us any closer to figuring out who killed the man," Salinger admitted. "The main reason I called you was to ask about Stubby."

"What about him?" I asked as I turned my head from side to side. My hair, damp with sweat, was falling out of my scrunchie and down my bare back. I leaned my ear against my shoulder to hold the phone in place so I could pull my hair back up.

"You told me that he's been seen around town with Pack Rat the past few weeks. Did you ever see him yourself?"

"No. I just know about him because several of the merchants I spoke to told me that he's been hanging around. Why? Do you suspect him?"

I adjusted the strap of my jog bra and returned to my stretching.

"Maybe," Salinger confided. "Several of the crimes James Baldwin was arrested for were carried out with an accomplice who fits the description you gave me of Stubby. We can't know for certain without fingerprints, but I'm guessing Stubby is really Lance Silverdale. Pack Rat and Stubby served in the war together and then seemed to hook up again after Pack Rat was freed. Lance has a rap sheet twice as long as Pack Rat's, with a lot more violent crimes thrown in. Lance was sent to prison in 1995, the same year Pack Rat moved here. I have to wonder if the two events are in some way related."

"What did Stubby go to prison for?" I asked.

"Armed robbery. He had an accomplice who got away. The men wore masks and the accomplice never was identified."

"So you're thinking Pack Rat was the accomplice?" I switched the phone over to my left hand and began stretching my right side.

"Maybe. It would explain why Pack Rat seemed to act as if he owed the guy something. If Stubby spent twenty years in prison without giving up his partner, I imagine that partner would feel pretty grateful."

"When did Stubby get out of prison?" I asked.

"Two months ago."

"I guess the timing fits. I wonder why Stubby came to Ashton Falls."

"I suppose he might have felt he was owed a debt. I'd really like to track this guy down to see what he knows."

I crossed my legs Indian style and thought about what Salinger had shared. It actually explained a lot. It explained why Pack Rat introduced Stubby around even though he was clearly uncomfortable doing so. If Stubby was staying in the campground that explained why Pack Rat had been going all the way out there. And if Pack Rat was doing Stubby's bidding as some sort of penance, it explained why his normal routine had been interrupted. I had to wonder whether Pack Rat knew that Stubby was stealing from the vendors he considered to be friends. Could he have found out and tried to stop him? Could this action have led to his death? And what had he been trying to sell?

"Jeremy said Pack Rat has been visiting a friend at the campground. It occurred to me just now that this friend might be Stubby," I informed Salinger. "I can go check it out after I get home and can pick up my truck."

"I'll go," Salinger insisted. "Zak will have my head if I let anything happen to you. I'll call you later to let you know what I find out."

"Okay. Then I guess I'll just continue with my jog."

"You do that. And Donovan . . ."

"Yeah?"

"Stay out of trouble."

I really did intend to do just that. I was going to finish my jog and head home, but somehow I found myself standing in front of the bar where I'd found Pack Rat's body. The place was situated in the middle of a fairly long block of businesses. To the right was a hair salon, to the left a video arcade. The hair salon would most likely have been closed at the time Pack Rat was murdered, but the arcade would have been open. I decided to head inside to see if anyone had seen anything on the night of the murder that would point us in a direction.

The arcade was quiet at this time of day. I knew that during the late afternoon and evening hours the noise made by all the bells and whistles would be deafening. Charlie and I headed toward the back of the building, where I noticed a maintenance man was working on one of the racing games. He was a man of medium height with greasy dark hair and an equally greasy work shirt.

"Can I help you?" he asked.

"My name is Zoe Donovan."

"Oh, you're Zak's girl. Heard you was gettin' married."

It figured Zak had been in here playing games. Sometimes my intelligent, sophisticated fiancé was such a child when it came to having fun.

"Yes, we are. Next Saturday. I was out jogging and happened to be passing by, and it occurred to me to stop by to ask if you were working last Friday evening. It would have been late in the evening."

"Yeah, I was here."

"Did you happen to notice a truck parked out in front of the bar next door?" I asked.

"Yeah, I seen it. Thing was a rusted-out piece of crap. I asked the guy to move it, but he said he was waitin' for someone and couldn't leave until his friend got there."

"Did he happen to mention the friend's name?" I asked.

"Nope. He didn't say. It looked like the guy got stood up, though. He was still sittin' in the truck when I left at the end of my shift."

"And what time was that?" I asked.

"Two a.m."

Pack Rat was probably already dead by then.

"Did you approach the truck at that time?"

"No. The guy had his hat over his face. I figured he was sleepin'. By that time the arcade was closed, so his sittin' there wasn't botherin' me."

A group of teens walked in and started pumping quarters into several nearby games. The noise level in the room rose considerably. I couldn't imagine how loud it must be when all the machines were going at once.

"What time would you say it was when you spoke to the man and asked him to move the truck?" I raised my voice to be heard over the noise.

"Guess about ten or eleven. Don't remember exactly, but I'd been on shift for a while when I noticed the truck, and I started at six."

"Did the man in the truck have the cowboy hat on when you spoke to him?"

The man thought about it. "No. In fact, I can't say I remember seein' it at all. Might have been in the back or on the floor."

I had to wonder if whoever killed Pack Rat had brought the hat. It really hadn't looked like something Pack Rat would wear.

"Did you notice anyone approach the truck that evening?" I asked.

The man paused to consider my question. "No, but I wasn't payin' attention. It was busy that night. Once I asked him to move the eyesore I didn't give it another thought until I left and saw it was still parked in the same spot. It was gone when I got here the next day."

I knew the truck had been gone by the time the man started work the next day because Salinger had had it towed.

"Had you noticed the man in the truck hanging around the area before?" I wondered.

"Nope." The man seemed sure of that. "I think I've seen him around town during the day, but I've never seen him at the bar and I don't recall seein' him after dark."

"Okay. Thank you for your time."

I turned to leave.

"Anytime. Say hi to Zak. It's been a while since he's been by. He used to come by on a real regular basis."

"He was out of town the past couple of weeks and now we have family in town for the wedding. I'm sure he'll be in once we get back from our honeymoon."

"You best tell him Kickstand is gettin' close to toppin' his high game on Hellrider." The man informed me like it was an urgent piece of information.

"Hellrider?"

"That game near the front door." The man pointed to a machine. "Zak has held the record for over a year, but Kickstand has been in here practicin' every day. Never seen someone so determined to steal the number-one spot."

I looked at the game the man had referred to. It was situated right in front of the front window.

"Was Kickstand here last Friday night?"

"Yeah. Never left the game until closin'."

"Do you think Kickstand'll be in later?"

"You can bet on it."

Maybe I could get Zak to come back with me later that afternoon. If Kickstand had been playing the game the man indicated he would have had a front-row view of Pack Rat's truck the entire evening. I supposed I could interview the man myself, but Zak would probably want the opportunity to defend his title while he was here.

Chapter 10

"Kickstand is fifteen?" I was having a hard time believing a fifteen-year-old was close to beating my video-game developing fiancé at a video game.

"And a girl," Zak verified.

"A fifteen-year-old girl is on the verge of breaking your high score?"

"Apparently."

I laughed. I hated to admit it, but I found I was rooting for the girl. Does that make me a horrible fiancé? Probably.

"Do you think she'll talk to us about what she saw on Friday night, if she did indeed see anything?" I asked as we shared a burger and fries at Ellie's place.

"Yeah." Zak folded a French fry into his mouth. "I think she will. It seems like she usually comes into the arcade at around five on weekdays." Zak looked at his watch. "It's one thirty, so we have a few hours to kill, unless you want to go back to the house."

"No. Levi said he and Scooter wouldn't be back until almost dark."

Levi had taken Scooter, Tucker, and the dogs hiking.

"And Alex is at Phyllis's again," I added, "so let's take advantage of the lull in family time to do something fun together. Just the two of us."

"Sounds good to me." Zak took my hand in his. "What would you like to do?"

Good question. I'd been running around like a chicken with its head cut off lately. I hadn't even had time to consider doing something just for fun. If we went back to the house one of the visiting family members would probably grab us, so we needed to think of something to do with the clothes and supplies we had on hand.

"I'm not sure. Let's finish our lunch and then decide. It's really nice to have a few minutes to ourselves. It seems like forever since we've even had a meal without half a dozen people present."

"It doesn't help that I had to go out of town to deal with the hacker," Zak admitted. "Which reminds me: I wanted to talk to you some more about the employment opportunity I offered him."

Zak had been out of town for the previous couple of weeks because of a problem one of his clients had been having with a hacker. It turned out the hacker had targeted that particular customer in order to get Zak's attention. He'd managed to stay one step ahead of Zak for over a week, so it turned out he was successful in doing just that. Once Zak caught up with him, he not only didn't have him arrested but he'd offered him a job.

The hacker was a sixteen-year-old high-school dropout and a computer savant. His name was Pi, and apparently Zak thought he was the best thing to happen to the software industry since Zak Zimmerman.

"So what about Pi?" I asked.

"I'd like to pay for his education."

I remembered Zak told me that he'd dropped out of high school after his mother died.

"He's much too advanced to get anything out of a public high school, so I'd like to see if I can talk him into a private school situation. He's living in foster care at the moment, so I'd like to apply to become his legal guardian so I can have a level of control over his educational and financial future."

"You want to adopt him?"

"No. Not adopt. It's more like I'd be his foster parent if I can get approval. That way I can make decisions on his behalf."

"Do you think he'll be okay with that?" I asked.

"I know he will. I've already talked to him about it. I volunteered to not only pay for him to get a high school diploma but a college degree as well. He's not totally into the whole going-back- to-school thing, but I told him that if he graduated college with a degree in computer science and stayed out of trouble between now and then, I'd give him a piece of my company and make him a partner."

"Are you sure about that?" I asked. "What if he isn't as smart as you think?"

"He kept me stumped for eight days using nothing more than an old laptop his foster parents let him use. The guy is brilliant. He deserves a chance."

I smiled. "Well, then, okay. I think your plan sounds really awesome. Is he going to work for you while he attends school?"

"That's the plan."

I took a sip of Zak's beer. It was nice to have a cool drink on a hot day. I had to admit that this man I was marrying was pretty amazing.

"You know," I said as I nibbled on the end of a salty fry, "if we keep collecting genius kids in need of private schooling, it might actually save us money just to build our own school like we talked about."

"I've been thinking about our conversation. Quite a lot, actually," Zak informed me. "The more I think about it, the more I like the idea. Not only would this provide us with the perfect situation for our own children when we have them but it would allow us to help other kids like Pi, Alex, and even Scooter."

"You know I've been worrying over the fact that Alex is worrying about going to high school next year," I said. "Did you have a chance to talk to her parents?"

He nodded. "They aren't sold on the particular school they're trying to work out admission for and are quite open to other options. They make a good point about the fact that she's outgrown the school she's been attending, though. Leaving her there for another year doesn't seem like a possibility."

"Are there other options to the high school?" I asked.

Zak placed his hand over mine and gave it a squeeze. "Maybe. I'm looking into a few things, but it would be premature to even talk about them at this point. I promise I'll figure something out."

I smiled. I trusted Zak and knew he'd do just that.

"In the meantime," Zak said, "I have something I want to show you. I was going to wait, but now seems like as good a time as any."

"What do you want to show me?" I asked.

"It's a surprise. I'll show you when we're done here."

"I'm done." I pushed my half-eaten burger across the table. I love surprises more than I love hamburgers.

"Okay, then. Let me pay the bill and we'll take a drive."

Zak took me on a long drive that took us up onto the mountain and then ended up less than five miles from our home. It was a beautiful drive, but I couldn't imagine why Zak had chosen a route that took over thirty minutes when the actual destination was less than five minutes from where we'd had lunch. When I asked him about it he said the anticipation of a surprise was half the fun and he wanted me to have the whole experience.

I'm marrying a crazy man.

"What do you think?" Zak asked as he stopped the truck on the side of the road.

I looked out over a large meadow that was backed by the tall mountain. The meadow had a natural lake with geese swimming across the smooth surface. It was an absolutely enchanting setting.

"It's beautiful," I said. "I've always really liked this meadow. Charlie and I use it as an access point to hike the mountain sometimes."

"It's not only beautiful, it's flat all the way up to the foothills," Zak commented.

"Yes, I can see that." I had no idea what my fiancé was getting at.

"And it's for sale. All seventy-eight acres, including the small lake."

"You want to buy this meadow?"

"It seemed like a good place to build a school, if we're really thinking of building a school."

"Are you serious?" I smiled.

"Completely. The land is close enough to town that we could easily accommodate kids who wanted to live at home and attend. And there's plenty of room to build both a school building and a dorm if there are students who want or need to board."

"Wow." I know we'd talked about the possibility of building a school, but that was only two days ago. I couldn't believe Zak had actually started looking at land. Were we crazy to even consider taking on such a huge project?

"I thought we'd start out small," Zak continued. "I've envisioned a two-story building with classrooms over there." He pointed to a location toward the back of the property, close to the mountain. "We could have the dorm to the left and a gymnasium to the far right. There would be plenty of room to expand once we got started."

"Wow; you've really thought this through."

"Yeah, I guess I have. Now that the idea has taken hold I'm really excited about it. We'll need help, though. Good and reliable help. Even though I do intend to slow down a bit and hire programmers to help with the projects I plan to take on over the next couple of years, I'll be away at least for short periods of time. And, although you have Jeremy and Tiffany to help out, you're still busy with the Zoo. I really think that if we're going to do this we'll need to hire someone to oversee the permit, building, and hiring processes."

I couldn't believe I was standing on the highway in a pair of cutoff jeans and flip-flops, discussing building a multimillion-dollar facility. This was all happening so fast. I looked at Zak. He seemed confident, and he was the smartest person I'd ever met. He was a millionaire many times over by the time he was twenty. He certainly wasn't one to sit on an idea once it took hold. My Zak was a doer. I should have known he'd be all over this.

"Do you have someone in mind to oversee the project?" I asked.

"Actually, I do. I spoke to Phyllis King. She's not only interested in helping with the planning and development of the project but she's expressed interest in running the facility once we get it open."

Zak was grinning at me like he'd just delivered me the moon. In a way, I guess he had. Not only could our own children live at home *and* get a top-rated education but as long as their parents' agreed to the plan, we could have Alex and Scooter close by as well.

I felt tears of happiness on my face as I threw myself into Zak's arms. "I think, yes, I want to do this. And I think, yes, you're the best fiancé in the world."

Kickstand, whose real name was Abby, was totally awesome. She was not only a video game ninja but she was outspoken, confident, and friendly. When Zak showed up and challenged her to a duel for high score, she didn't bat an eye. I should have felt bad that everyone in the video arcade was rooting for Kickstand, including me, but I could tell by the gleam in Zak's eye that while he wouldn't throw the game, he was rooting for her as well.

I think the fact that Zak understands that Abby wants to earn top score and not be handed top score is what will make Zak an awesome father. He's observant and insightful when it comes to dealing with the younger humans in his life. I'm sure that's why he's able to work so well with kids like Scooter, who was such a mess when Zak was first introduced to him. I really didn't think he was salvageable based on his attitude and deviant behavior. But Zak saw something in him that no one else did, and he had him acting like a civilized kid within a couple of days.

I had no doubt Zak would make an equally positive impact on Pi's life. The kid was smart and obviously determined. He'd sent Zak an application for employment, and when Zak hadn't responded, instead of giving up, he'd hacked into the computer system of one of Zak's best clients to show him what he could do. Anyone else would most likely have had the boy arrested. But not Zak. Zak saw the potential in people and knew how to bring out the best in those he took an interest in.

I found that my heart was beating rapidly while I watched Zak and Kickstand fight for the lead. It was a very close game, and the lead changed hands several times during the course of the hour the duel was in play. Both contestants had sweat on their foreheads as they fought for hard-earned points. In the end Zak won, but not by a lot.

"Awesome game." Zak gave the girl a high five.

"I'll get you next time," she challenged.

"You know," Zak winked, "you just might at that."

I cleared my throat to remind Zak that we were there to talk to her about Pack Rat.

"How about you let Zoe and me take you to dinner?" Zak offered. "Anywhere you want to go."

"Isn't the loser supposed to buy?" Kickstand asked.

"Not when the loser cut the winner some slack so as not to embarrass him in front of his girlfriend."

That comment earned Zak a huge grin and an agreement to come to dinner.

After we were settled on pizza, Zak went to the counter to order our dinner while Abby and I found a table.

As soon as we sat down, I had to ask her the question that had been on my mind since I'd met her. "Why Kickstand?"

The girl shrugged. "My dad started calling me that when I was a little kid. My mom was sick, and I have three brothers and a sister. My dad worked a lot, so I was left to take care of things at home. My dad said I was the one who held everything together and supported everyone. He said that if our family was a bike, I would be the kickstand that kept the whole thing from crashing to the ground."

"Aw. That's sweet."

"My dad is awesome."

"And your mom? Is she better?" I asked.

"She died last year."

"I'm so sorry."

Abby shrugged.

"Do you still have to take care of your younger siblings?"

"No. My sister and two youngest brothers went to live with my aunt and uncle after Mom died. It's just dad and me and my thirteen-year-old brother Darmon now. Dad still works a lot and Darmon has his own thing, so I hang out at the arcade."

"You must really miss your younger siblings," I sympathized.

"I guess. It is what it is. You got any kids?"

"No. Zak and I aren't married yet."

"Figured. It's just that I saw you in town the other day with a girl with dark hair."

"That's Alex. She's staying with us for a few weeks."

"Lucky girl. You have a great house."

I couldn't help but see the longing in Abby's eyes.

"Why don't you come over tomorrow? The kids who are visiting for the wedding are all younger than you, but you might still enjoy the pool. One of Zak's cousins is seventeen and she's pretty nice, and Alex is only ten, but she's really mature."

Abby shrugged. "Maybe. If I'm not busy." While she tried to act nonchalant, I could see a little half smile that she tried to hide.

"Be warned, Scooter and his friend Tucker can get pretty rowdy."

"I know Scooter. He's a punk, but he's okay."

"You know Scooter?" I was surprised, considering the five-year age difference.

"Before he moved he used to hang out in the arcade. We hung out sometimes while the other kids were in school."

"You guys cut class together?"

"Sometimes. School is boring. Seems like a waste of time, if you ask me."

"You don't want to go to college?" I asked.

"Yeah, college looks like fun, but there's no way my dad could afford it, so I don't really see the point in finishing high school."

"The point is," Zak commented as he joined us after ordering the food, "that an education opens doors, while the lack of one closes them. I thought you wanted to be a video game developer."

"I do."

"Then you'll need an education."

Abby picked up the soda Zak had set in front of her. She took a long drink. "Did you go to college?" she asked him.

"Actually, I didn't. But that doesn't mean you shouldn't."

"Maybe."

"If you want to develop video games Zak has a friend who does that for a living. You should definitely come by tomorrow," I said. "Maybe she can give you some tips."

Abby peered over the top of her glass suspiciously. "What games?"

"Zombie Slayer, for one," I answered.

"Get out. The person who developed Zombie Slayer is at your house?"

"Her name is Isabella and I think the two of you would get along just fine."

Abby smiled.

"So, I was wondering if you were at the arcade on Friday night," Zak said after the waiter brought our pizza.

"Yeah. So?"

"Do you remember seeing a beat-up old truck parked in front of the bar next door?"

Abby looked at Zak suspiciously. "So this whole pizza thing was just so you could ask me about the dead guy?"

"Not just," Zak defended himself.

"Geez. I should have known."

"I really am enjoying our conversation and I really do want you to come by the house tomorrow," I began. "But the guy who died was a friend of mine, and we're just trying to find out what happened to him."

Abby looked at me, then at Zak. "Can I get a refill?"

"Refills are free," Zak informed her.

Zak and I waited while Abby crossed the room to the soda fountain.

"Do you think she knows anything?" I whispered to Zak.

"She might. I think if she didn't, she'd just come out and say so. I'd be willing to bet her refill is a stall tactic so she can think it through. Here she comes."

Abby sat down across from us. She looked at us for a minute before she spoke. "Yeah, I saw the truck," she eventually offered. "The old guy who died was sitting in it."

"Did you see anyone else near the truck?" Zak asked.

"Couple of people."

"Can you describe them?" Zak persuaded.

Abby took a drink of her soda. She picked a corner off the crust of the pizza and popped it in her mouth. I wasn't sure if she was stalling for dramatic effect, but all we could do was wait.

"When the truck first pulled up there was this short guy with one arm in the passenger seat," Abby began as she nibbled on a piece of pepperoni. "He went into the bar. The old guy who died waited in the truck. For a long time," Abby emphasized. "After a while Chet came out and said something to the guy in the truck."

"Chet?" I asked.

"He's the bartender," Abby informed me.

I looked at Zak. "Do you know this Chet?"

"Big guy with a tattoo of Pooh Bear on his arm?"

"Yeah, that's him," Abby verified.

"Pooh Bear?" I asked.

Abby shrugged. "The guy likes bears."

"The bar must have been busy on a Friday night. Did you see anyone else approach the truck?" I asked.

"No. I'm not saying no one did, I'm just saying I didn't notice. There were a lot of people coming and going. A couple of big groups loitered out in front of the bar before going in. I guess one of them might have talked to the guy. Like I said, I wasn't paying that much attention. The truck was still there when I left at around midnight, though, and it seems like the guy with one arm might still have been inside."

Zak asked her some additional questions. I wasn't sure any of this information would help us, but it gave us a starting point. Or, more accurately, it would give Salinger a starting point. Zak absolutely insisted that we call the sheriff with the information and let him follow up. We were, after all, getting married in less than seventy-two hours.

The first thing I noticed when we arrived home was the topless woman doing yoga on the beach.

"Nona?" I asked.

"Yup."

"She do this often?"

Zak shrugged.

"Zachary," the tall, lean woman crossed the sand with her arms held out for a hug.

Zak opened his arms and hugged the woman back. I looked around for the kids; luckily, they were nowhere in sight. Levi must have taken them to the boathouse, like he'd said he might.

"And this must be Zoe." The woman locked me in a death grip. I had to admit, the woman wasn't shy.

"I'm happy to meet you." I tried not to stare at the half-naked woman who seemed to be in remarkable shape for her age.

Nona looked me up and down. "I have a good feeling about this one," Nona said to Zak. "The planets are nicely aligned and Helen is in retrograde."

"Retrograde?"

"You've dealt with her nicely. Not everyone can. Now, where did I put that scotch?"

Zak wrapped a large beach towel around Nona's shoulders. "Maybe you should come in. It's going to be dark soon, and it normally gets chilly when the sun goes down."

"Nonsense. The night has just begun. I think I'll go for a swim."

"Is anyone else here?" I asked as Nona began to strip down to nothing.

"No. Jimmy was lurking about, but he left when I decided to begin my yoga. A delicious young man with gorgeous dark hair stopped by with the children. I tried to speak to him, but he turned around and left as soon as he got here."

I looked at Zak. He smiled sheepishly. I nodded toward the naked woman approaching our pool. He shrugged.

"I guess I'll go pick up the kids," I announced. "Zak will find you something comfortable to wear while I'm gone."

"Of course, dear. I understand completely."

I sincerely doubted it. I just hoped she wouldn't traumatize poor Scooter. When Zak told me that we'd have to choose between Nona and Helen as our houseguest I'd thought Nona the better choice. Now I wasn't so sure.

Chapter 11

I was pretty much convinced Stubby had something to do with Pack Rat's death, so I'd agreed with Zak that it was best to let Salinger track him down. It appeared Stubby had asked Pack Rat to drive him to the bar and then wait for him in the truck. He must have known that, as a recovering alcoholic, he wouldn't want to go inside, which would leave him poised for whomever came along and injected him with the air. It seemed like a perfectly reasonable theory until Salinger called to inform me that Stubby had been found dead in the campground, along with a tent full of things he'd stolen from merchants in town.

"So now what?" I asked Zak as we kept an eye on the pool full of kids. Luckily, Abby—I refused to call her Kickstand, and for some reason she was giving me a pass—and Alex hit it off despite their age difference, and Scooter and Tucker were having as much fun as they'd had every day that week. I had a feeling Tucker would miss Scooter when he returned to school.

"Now we enjoy the afternoon while we can, before we need to get ready for the rehearsal dinner my mom has planned," Zak answered as a huge splash of water hit us in the face.

"No more cannonballs," Zak called to the boys, who had decided to have a competition to see who could splash the most water out of the pool. Even Twyla's pair weren't as wound up as Scooter and Tucker today.

"Are you sure we have to go to this dinner?" I asked.

"I'm sure. Mom booked the entire back room at the Wharf."

"Did she at least invite Levi and Ellie?"

"I saw to it personally," Zak assured me.

"And how are we going to deal with the Nona-and-your-mom situation?"

"Alcohol."

"We're going to get them drunk?" I asked. That actually sounded like a pretty good idea. Thankfully, Nona had retired to her room by the time I got home with Alex and Scooter the previous evening and hadn't come out as of yet, but based on her comments I could see that getting the two women together in one room might not be the best idea.

"No, the alcohol is for us," Zak teased. "I figure we'll need it in large quantities to deal with the circus that's certain to ensue once everyone gets together."

I laughed. "You never get drunk. Besides, we'll have the kids." At least I'd been assuming we would. "We will have the kids, won't we?"

"Yes, they're invited."

"And you're sure we absolutely can't get out of this?"

Zak didn't bother to respond.

"We aren't actually practicing the ceremony, are we?" I asked.

"No. I managed to convince my mom that the two of us had already practiced."

I blushed as I remembered our rehearsal the previous week. "I hope you didn't go into detail."

"I did not."

"And for the actual ceremony, we're going to let Pastor Dan do all the talking while we just say I do?"

Initially, Zak had wanted us to write our own vows, but I'm not really very good at things like that, so he'd agreed to a traditional ceremony in which the pastor did all the talking.

"Yes. I've spoken to Dan, and he assured me you don't have to speak at all. A simple nod will suffice."

I laced my fingers through Zak's. "I think I can manage to say *I do*, although if I get totally tongue-tied I have a few ideas of how to demonstrate my intent."

"You know," Zak leaned over and kissed me on the lips, "all this talk about vows is giving me ideas of a different kind."

I glanced toward the poolful of kids. "You're the one who volunteered us to do lifeguard duty."

Zak groaned. "Yeah, I guess I did at that."

I leaned back in my lounge chair and watched the kids as they laughed and splashed around. I couldn't believe it was already Thursday. I'd been certain I'd never make it until the wedding without strangling at least one Zimmerman family member or friend, but here it was, two short days until the big day, and I hadn't even raised my voice. Much.

"Did you speak to Nona about nude yoga on the beach?" I asked.

"I reminded her that we had children staying with us, and she assured me that she understood completely."

"Has she always been so . . ."

"Free-spirited? No. In fact, she used to be quite a bitter old lady who made it her mission to make everyone else miserable."

"And what happened?"

"Honestly, we aren't sure. One night about ten years ago she went to bed an unhappy old woman and the next morning she woke up a free-spirited hippie. The doctors are fairly certain she had a stroke of some sort, but other than the complete change in personality, she seems fine."

"Maybe she was possessed by the love child of Christmas Past," I teased.

"Maybe. All I know is that she tossed out her stodgy clothes and iron rod, bought a Harley, took up yoga, and set out to experience the world."

"Cindy told me that Nona is the trustee who ensures that the specific stipulations outlined in her late husband's will are adhered to. Keeping track of how many nights Eric and Cindy spend together seems at odds with her new lease on life."

"It does seem odd. She's a totally different person in every other way, but she still rules over Eric like he's a brainless child. I think she sees his weaknesses and hopes she can find a way to get him to grow up a bit before he receives the bulk of his money."

"The whole thing seems archaic to me."

"Yeah, I guess it is."

Darlene walked out of the house and handed me my phone. "You left this on the kitchen table. It was ringing. I thought it might be important."

"Thanks." I smiled at the girl as I took the phone from her outstretched hand. I checked it, and the only missed call was from an unknown number. Most likely a telemarketer. I thought about calling the number back but decided it could wait.

"Anything important?" Zak asked.

"Unknown number. They didn't leave a message. I hadn't realized it was so late. I guess we should think about what we're going to feed all these people for lunch."

"I guess if you want to hold down the fort I can go to the deli and pick up sandwiches," Zak offered.

"How about you hold down the fort and I'll pick up the food? I'll call in an order so it's ready when I get there. And Zak—don't leave the kids alone with Nona."

"Don't worry. I'll keep an eye on things."

I called in the order, then changed into shorts and a tank top, grabbed Charlie, and headed into town. It was a beautiful summer day, much like every other beautiful summer day in Ashton Falls, but for some reason the sky seemed a little bluer, the lake a little clearer, and the flowers just a bit more colorful. No doubt about it: I was happy.

As I drove through town toward the deli I passed the spot where I'd found Pack Rat's body. The bar was closed, but I noticed a big guy with a Pooh Bear tattoo speaking to another person in front of the open door. I pulled my truck over to the curb. Abby had told Zak and me that Chet had come out to the truck to speak to Pack Rat on the night he died. Maybe he remembered something that could help us track down the killer.

I got out of the truck and approached the men. The man Chet had been speaking to continued down the street as I neared.

"Chet?" I asked.

"Yeah. Who's asking?"

"Zoe Donovan. I heard you were on shift the night Pack Rat Nelson died in front of the bar. I wondered if you saw or heard anything that might help us track down the killer."

"You a cop?"

"No. Not exactly. I'm more of a consultant."

Chet looked me up and down. "Consultant?"

"Yeah. I help Sheriff Salinger with murder investigations from time to time. On the night in question, did you speak to Pack Rat?"

"I came out to tell him to move his eyesore of a truck from in front of the bar. The guy said he was waiting for someone and refused to go. Technically, he was legally parked, so there wasn't a lot I could do about it and I went back inside."

"Do you remember seeing someone at the bar that evening with one arm? He was a short man who went by the name of Stubby."

Chet shrugged. "I might have. I'm not sure. I don't know all the customers who come through and we were busy that night, so I wasn't taking the time to stop and chat."

"Have you seen a man fitting that description in the bar on other occasions?"

"I can't say that I have." Chet answered.

"Did you approach the truck after you finished your shift?" I wondered

"No. I left through the back door because I was parked in the alley. Now, if you're done *consulting* I really need to get inside."

"Sure. No problem. Thank you for your help."

I continued on to the deli. The street in front of the building was packed with cars that had been parked along the street before their occupants headed to the beach, so I took a shortcut I knew of and headed down the alley. As a rule, only the proprietors who had businesses along Main were supposed to park in the alley, but I knew Gilda only used one of her two allotted spaces and I figured she wouldn't mind letting me borrow her employee parking for the few minutes it would take me to walk around to the front, enter the deli, and pick up the food.

When I drove past Sprinkles I noticed a brand-new bear-proof Dumpster had been installed, and I knew a similar can had been installed at the Taco Hut as well. Now that the entire alley was covered the bears would have to find somewhere else to scavenge.

I pulled into Gilda's extra spot and turned off the ignition. All at once I was hit with a wave of emotion, realizing that Pack Rat would no longer be a presence in the alley the way he'd been for as long as I could remember. I knew Zak was right; we really did need to let Salinger handle things, but I felt so helpless going to fancy dinners in my honor when there was a killer on the loose. I glanced in my rearview mirror and spotted the most pathetic dog I'd ever seen sitting near the Dumpster behind me. I told Charlie to stay as I slowly exited the truck. I had to be careful not to scare the poor thing off. Not only was its coat, which I believed had once been white, filthy and matted but he was so skinny his ribs were clearly visible.

I kept a stash of dog treats in my truck for just such occasions. I grabbed a handful of them and a lead and carefully made my way toward the frightened animal. I walked as slowly as possible, maintaining eye contact with him the entire time.

"Hey there, sweet boy. Are you hungry?"

The dog looked directly at the treats in my hand. I could tell he was interested but reluctant to move.

"Don't be scared. I'm not going to hurt you."

The dog began to whine.

"If you come with me I'll feed you and get you all cleaned up."

The dog lay down on the pavement. He didn't run, but he didn't approach me either, and it seemed to me as if he was watching me in fear, although his tail wagged just a tiny bit.

I walked slowly forward until I was close enough to offer him a dog treat. He cautiously took it from my hand. I set several more on the ground in front of him, which gave me the opportunity to place the lead around his neck. When he'd been secured I noticed he was sitting on something blue. Upon further investigation, I realized it was a large man's shirt. I'd seen Pack Rat wearing one exactly like it not that long ago.

"Are you waiting for Pack Rat?" I asked the dog.

It appeared that was exactly what he'd been doing.

"Have you been waiting here all week?"

The dog whined. I tried to lead him to the truck, but he sat down on the shirt and refused to move. I bribed the dog to take a step forward with the last of the treats in my pocket and then bent over and picked up the shirt when he'd stepped away from it.

"We can bring the shirt," I promised him.

The dog looked at me with huge sad eyes. I felt my heart break at his obvious distress.

"I know. I miss him too."

I knelt down and petted the filthy dog before I slowly led him toward the truck. I placed the shirt on my backseat and then boosted the poor animal into the truck. I watched as Charlie greeted him enthusiastically, but he didn't seem all that interested. The poor thing looked as if he were completely depressed.

I took out my phone and called Zak. I told him about the dog and the fact that I really needed to take him to the Zoo. Zak agreed to have Darlene watch the kids while he ran into town and picked up the food.

"Maybe you should ask Darlene to get the food in case Nona wakes up," I suggested.

"Yeah. She promised she'd behave, but it might be best if I stayed to keep an eye on things."

"I'll be back as soon as I can," I promised.

"Go ahead and do what you need to do. I've got this," Zak reassured me.

Have I mentioned that I have the best fiancé ever?

"I can't believe this is the same dog I found behind the Dumpster," I said to Jeremy a couple of hours later, after the animal had been fed and bathed.

"He does look better," Jeremy agreed.

"He seems happier as well. I'm sure he misses Pack Rat, but maybe he just needed to know that he had someone to take care of him."

It always made my heart glad to be able to help out a four-legged friend.

"Scott is going to stop by in a bit to take a look at him," Jeremy informed me. "If he checks out, I guess we should start thinking about what you want to do with him."

"I'm certain he's been a stray for a while, considering his overall condition, but we should still do our due diligence and post a notice that he's been found. If no one responds let's find him a really good home. He seems to be in mourning over Pack Rat. Maybe we can place him with an older man who likes to take lots of walks."

"What about Mr. Hanover?" Jeremy suggested.

Mr. Hanover was a retired mailman who had adopted two of our kittens the previous October. He was a kind and patient man, and as of the last time I'd spoken to him, he didn't have a dog. He liked to take walks, he lived alone, and he had a house with a fenced yard.

I bent over and scratched the dog behind the ears. He wagged his tail in a sort of half wag, like he simply couldn't muster the energy for a full one.

"Let's see how this little guy is with cats; if he likes them then I think Mr. Hanover would be perfect," I decided.

"I think he's been through enough today. I'll try introducing him to some of the younger cats tomorrow. We have those two that came in a couple of weeks ago that seem to do okay with dogs."

"Okay, that sounds like a good idea. When Scott gets here ask him about food dosage. The poor thing needs to be fattened up, but we don't want to upset his digestive system."

"What do you want me to do with that old shirt?" Jeremy asked.

The shirt was filthy and really should be tossed, but I knew the dog found comfort in it. I definitely remembered seeing Pack Rat wearing it. At first I wasn't certain, but then I saw the patch on the elbow of one arm. It was pretty distinctive, and I definitely remembered seeing Pack Rat wearing that exact shirt on more than one occasion.

"Let's put it in the pen with the dog," I suggested. "He seems to be really attached to it. I'm sure it smells like his buddy."

Jeremy picked the shirt up off the ground. "There's something in the pocket." He handed me a folded piece of paper that had a list of words and numbers on it. I had no idea what they meant, but my instinct told me that they might be important. I wanted to take it to show it to Salinger, but I was already going to be late for my rehearsal dinner, so I put the paper in my pocket and headed for home.

Chapter 12

As I sat in the middle of the restaurant and surveyed the carnage left by Twyla's children, I found myself vowing never to have any of the destructive little parasites of my own. Darlene had tried to warn me, but they'd been so good since they'd been here that I'd thought she'd been exaggerating. Of course I hadn't been around much the past few days, so maybe I'd been gleefully ignorant of what really had been going on.

"We're going to be banned from this restaurant forever," I complained to Ellie. "And I do so love their scampi."

"I overheard Zak offer to pay for both the cleanup and all of the damage," Ellie informed me. "I'm pretty sure he's slipped the guy a couple of hundreds already. It'll be fine."

"Where is Zak anyway?" I asked.

Ellie shrugged. "My best guess is that he's cleaning out his bank account to pay for all of this. I'm pretty sure those kids managed to break at least one dish from every table. How is that even possible?"

I ducked as a plate of mashed potatoes flew past my head. "That's how."

"Someone needs to do something," Ellie insisted. "Where's their mother?"

I looked around the dining room for Twyla. She was sitting at the bar with the cousins, nursing a drink as if nothing unusual was happening. Zak's mother was sitting at a table with her friend Susan. They were in deep conversation and likewise ignoring the children. Nona had decided to skip the dinner in favor of having drinks with a man no older than forty who she'd picked up in the parking lot as we were walking into the restaurant. Isabella seemed to have disappeared.

"We still have to get through dessert." I groaned. "And speeches. For some reason Zak's mom is insisting on speeches."

"Maybe we can tie them up until it's time to leave," Levi offered.

"They're children. We can't tie them up," I said. "Can we?" I looked at Ellie.

"We can't," she confirmed.

"I'll see if I can get them to behave," Alex volunteered. "For some reason they like me."

"Oh, honey. It's too dangerous. I can't send you into battle alone."

"I'll take Scooter."

Scooter and Alex were sitting at a table with Levi, Ellie, Zak before he'd left, and me.

"Are you crazy?" Scooter complained.

"It'll be fine." Alex took Scooter's hand and led him across the room.

I saw her say something to the pair of children responsible for all the destruction. I was expecting bloodshed and was prepared to hurry to her aid, but both children—who, if I remembered correctly, were four and six—seemed to be listening to her. There was an exchange of words and then the pair followed Alex and Scooter over to a table in the corner. Alex continued to speak to them and they continued to sit quietly and listen. Even Scooter seemed to be hanging on her every word.

"What do you think she's saying to them?" Ellie asked.

"I don't know, but whatever it is, it's working. They seem to be completely entranced."

"She's like some sort of child whisperer."

"I bet she's telling them a story. Did you know Alex is writing a book? Phyllis told me it's really very good."

"A book? Isn't she only ten?"

"In the short time I've known Alex I've learned that her age is not a limitation."

Ellie, Levi, and I watched as Zak came back into the room with Isabella trailing behind him. He said something to his mother, who nodded. He then went over to the bar and spoke to the cousins. Twyla said something to Zak that looked a lot like a complaint, but eventually all the cousins got up from where they were sitting. Twyla walked over to where her children were sitting, took them by the hand, and led them out of the building. Then he returned to our table with Alex and Scooter.

"They're leaving?" I asked.

"We all are. I think I've had about as much fun as I'm up for."

"I'm sorry the kids ruined your dinner," Ellie sympathized.

"It wasn't my dinner. It was Mrs. Zimmerman's dinner. I didn't even want to have it." I looked at Zak. "Is she mad?"

"Oddly, she isn't. I think even she was ready for the circus to be over."

I turned and looked at Alex. "What did you say to them? They seemed to settle right down as soon as you started talking to them."

"They were just bored, so I told them a story. I'm not sure it's their fault they got into trouble. All the adults weren't paying any attention to them, so they were left to entertain themselves. Maybe we should hire someone to keep an eye on them during the wedding."

I put one arm around Alex and the other around Scooter and hugged them both. "You guys are so awesome. Thank you so much for helping."

I looked at Zak. "Nona rode over with us. Should we find her to tell her we're leaving?"

"I spoke to her before I came back into the dining room. Her date assured me he would see her home, and she told me not to wait up."

I couldn't help but laugh. The old gal certainly kept things interesting.

Later that evening, after I'd gotten the kids into bed, I curled up on the love seat in our bedroom and studied the piece of paper I'd found in Pack Rat's pocket. Zak was in his office having a telephone conversation with Pi, who appeared to be interested in Zak's proposal, and Levi and Ellie had gone home, as had the cousins and out-of-town guests. Nona still wasn't home, and if I had to guess, I'd say we most likely wouldn't be seeing her until the morning.

The note consisted of a series of letters and numbers. At first it didn't make any sense, but the more I studied it, the more I realized the scribbles appeared to be related to the robberies on Main Street. I might not have been able to put the rough code together if I hadn't spoken to the merchants. There were six rows of entries. The first row said: S- B08 – T 12 – R14 and S 6. Suzie had mentioned that she'd found $40 in her scarf basket and the numbers added up to 40. There was a checkmark next to the entry. I suspected that the letter in front of the number represented the item taken.

On the next line was: P-B15 – R05. I assumed the P stood for Pam and the dollar amount was equal to the value of the stolen items.

Each line below that followed the pattern. The first four lines had checkmarks next to them. The last two, which I assumed were for Bears and Beavers and Outback Hunting and Fishing, due to the fact that one line started with a B and the last line with an O, did not.

"I think I figured out the code," I said to Zak when he walked into the room after completing his call. "I'm guessing this is an inventory of what was stolen from the merchants on Main Street, along with the estimated value of the items."

I showed Zak the paper.

"Both Suzie and Trish reported finding money after the break-ins. Horton and Gilda didn't. If you look at the list, Gilda was the second to the last victim and Horton was the last. They aren't checked off."

"So you think Pack Rat was stealing stuff and then leaving the money for it a few days later?" Zak said.

"I think *Stubby* was stealing stuff and Pack Rat was leaving money for it a few days later."

"Why would Stubby steal a salt and pepper set?"

"I have no idea, but it's the only thing that makes sense. Everyone I've spoken to reported that Pack Rat didn't seem to want to introduce Stubby around. It was more like he was compelled to for some reason. Salinger mentioned that they were in Vietnam together, and that after Pack Rat returned home he hooked up with Stubby and temporarily entered a life of crime. My guess is that either Pack Rat owed Stubby a debt of some sort or Stubby was blackmailing him with something he knew. In either case, Pack Rat felt he had no choice but to introduce Stubby around. When he saw Stubby was stealing from his friends he decided to pay for the items."

"Where did Pack Rat get the money to do that?" Zak asked.

"Kelly said he talked about needing to sell some stuff. He never sold anything, but I'm willing to bet that in this case he felt selling and paying for the merchandise his friend stole was his only option."

"Did all the store owners who are checked off find money?"

I looked at the list. There were four names checked off. Or at least there were codes for four names. I was sure S was Second Hand Suzie's, T was Trish's Treasures, P was Pam's Posies, and M was Margie at Mountain Sportswear. All four of those businesses shared space in the old town section of Ashton Falls, along with Bears and Beavers and Outback Hunting and Fishing. I hadn't asked Pam about the break-ins when I was in her store with Alex, and I haven't seen Margie in several weeks. Suddenly I knew what was on my agenda for the following day.

Chapter 13

The next morning I managed to convince Zak that I had some last-minute wedding stuff to take care of and would need to meet him at the picnic his mom had planned for the family. What I really wanted to do was follow up on a couple of hunches I had regarding Pack Rat's murder, but I was afraid if I told Zak what I intended to do, he'd try to talk me out of investigating the day before the wedding.

Not that I would blame him. It did seem like I'd needed a lot of rescuing of late.

"Damn," I muttered after climbing into my truck and searching through my backpack.

"Problem?" Nona, who had just pulled up on her Harley, asked.

"I wanted to do a few things in town, but I think Zak might still have my truck keys from last night. I guess I'll have to see if I can track down the spares."

"Hop on." Nona patted the leather seat behind her. "I'll give you a lift."

I looked at the bike. I knew I shouldn't trust the geriatric hippie to keep me safe, but I really wanted to ride on that pink bike.

"I have several stops to make," I warned her.

"I'm not busy."

Was I insane to even consider this?

"I don't have a helmet."

"You can wear mine. My old noggin is so rattled there's really very little risk of harming it more."

"Okay," I unwisely decided. "I guess it could be fun."

I climbed onto Nona's backseat, knowing all the while that I was an idiot for doing so. At least Nona was completely clothed today, in black leather pants, black leather boots, her pink leather jacket, and a pink tank top, and she looked surprisingly good considering she had to be close to eighty.

"Where are we heading?" Nona asked.

"Pam's Posies. It's in the center of town."

"Hang on."

Nona gunned the engine and took off in a flash. If not for the bar behind my back I would have fallen off for sure. I knew within the first half second that deciding to ride with Nona was probably the last thing I would ever do. But, hey, what a way to go.

I screamed as Nona slid around a tight corner. This was both the most awesome and most terrifying ride of my life. I tried to tell her that she might want to slow down, but she was laughing, or more accurately cackling, so loudly that I was certain she hadn't heard me.

I felt the contents of my stomach slowly make their way upward through my digestive system. It's not that I haven't ridden on a motorcycle before. Levi has one, and I'd ridden with him on many occasions. It was more that I hadn't ridden on a motorcycle with a septuagenarian with a death wish.

"I think I'm going to puke," I warned Nona just as we screeched to a halt in front of Pam's Posies.

I pulled off the helmet and took several deep breaths. My legs felt like jelly as I dismounted the death trap.

"Give it a minute; it'll pass," Nona assured me.

I felt the color slowly return to my face as I handed Nona her helmet.

"Thanks for the ride," I said. "I'm sure I can catch a ride home with Ellie. I might be a while and I'd hate to ask you to wait."

"Nonsense. I'm happy to wait. In fact, I'll come in with you."

Terrific.

"Nothing like an open-air ride to chase the cobwebs from your brain," Nona declared.

I was pretty sure that after the ride I'd just taken my brain was completely dust free.

It was still early and Pam's wasn't yet crowded. I followed Nona into the colorful shop, praying all the while that she'd behave herself and not decide that naked yoga among the flowers was the best idea she'd had all day.

"Did you come for your flowers?" Pam asked.

"Yes." I looked at Nona. "I mean, no. I was going to pick them up, but I came into town with Nona. I'll come back for them later."

Pam looked out the window. "That your pink Harley?"

"That's my girl," Nona confirmed.

"Nice." Pam turned her attention back to me. "If you aren't here for the flowers, what can I help you with?"

"I wanted to ask you a few questions about the rash of burglaries over the past couple of weeks."

"You heard about them, did you? Yeah, I got hit. About ten days ago."

"Did you report it?" I asked.

"I was going to, but all that was taken was a basket and some ribbon. It didn't seem worth the effort. Besides, two days later someone left a twenty next to my cash register."

"I don't suppose you happen to sell medicinal plants?" Nona asked.

Pam looked confused.

"She doesn't sell marijuana, Nona." I sighed.

She shrugged. "Can't blame a girl for asking."

Pam looked at me and frowned. I gave her a weak smile.

"It looks like the thief was Stubby," I informed Pam.

"Pack Rat's friend?"

"Yeah. I doubt he was really after a basket and ribbon. Do you have any idea why he might have broken in here?" I asked.

"Not a one. I can't imagine what someone like Stubby would want with anything I have. The break-in occurred after-hours. I don't leave money on the premises overnight. He didn't strike me as the sort to be in to flower arranging."

"When Pack Rat first introduced you to Stubby did he seem uncomfortable about doing so?" I wondered.

I watched Nona as she walked around the store sniffing candles. As crazy as it seemed, I found myself hoping she wasn't planning to shoplift anything. I'm not sure why I thought that was something she might do, but it just seemed to fit her overall personality.

"Yeah. I could tell Pack Rat didn't really like the guy. I'm not sure why he bothered to show him around. I got the feeling the one-armed guy had some sort of hold over Pack Rat. Like maybe he owed him a favor, or maybe he was afraid of him for some reason."

"When Pack Rat brought Stubby by did you notice him showing any particular interest in anything? Did he ask any questions?"

"He wanted to use the bathroom. He was gone for a long time too. Do you think he was casing the place?"

"Maybe. Did he come around again after that first time?" I asked.

"I saw him in the alley, but no, he didn't come inside."

After we finished speaking to Pam, Nona and I went next door to speak to Margie at Mountain Sportswear. She reported the same thing everyone else had: Pack Rat had brought Stubby around a few weeks ago, but he hadn't seemed happy about doing so. Margie had only spoken briefly to Stubby on that first occasion and had only seen him in passing since then. She also reported that her place had been broken in to and, like the others, only a few small items had been taken. I asked her if she'd found any money lying around afterward, and she said she hadn't. I remembered her name had been crossed off on the paper, so I looked around for a possible location for Pack Rat to have left some cash. After a short search we found the money tucked into an inventory journal Margie kept near the cash register.

"Seems like this Stubby was casing the joint so he could break in later," Nona commented after we returned to the Harley.

"Exactly."

It was scary that the crazy lady and I were on the same page.

"But why steal random meaningless stuff?" I asked.

"To divert attention from the real reason for the break-in," Nona declared.

"Stubby took stuff so everyone would assume it was just a burglary and wouldn't look any further for a purpose behind the break-in."

"Sounds like a theory to me." Nona nodded.

"Okay, but why these specific businesses?" I asked. "Both Jim at the Taco Hut and Ernie at the market reported that Pack Rat had been by and introduced Stubby, but they weren't robbed."

Nona looked around. "The taco place is down the street."

"Yeah, and the market is around the corner."

"Proximity."

I frowned.

"All the businesses that were broken in to were right next to one another," Nona pointed out.

"You're right. The common link has to be the building. I wonder what he was after."

"It seems it has to be something unique to the building," Nona said. "Anything stand out about this particular property?"

I thought about it. The building was old. It was one of the ones preserved from when Ashton Montgomery had bought Devil's Den and redeveloped the area. Both Jim's Taco Hut and Ernie's market were housed in buildings that had been built in the past twenty years.

"I need to go back to Pack Rat's cabin," I decided. "I have a vague memory of something catching my eye when I was there a few days ago, before I got distracted by the cat. My Zodar is telling me that it might be a clue."

"Hop on. I'll give you a lift," Nona offered.

There was a voice in my head telling me that it made more sense for me to head over to Ellie's to borrow her car or have her give me a ride home so I could get my own, but apparently Nona's crazy driving had chased all the sense from my brain because I found myself climbing on her death trap of a machine one more time.

I closed my eyes and gave myself over to the thrill of the ride.

"Woo wee. That's a lot of stuff," Nona sang out as we pulled up to the cabin.

"Guess that's why everyone called him Pack Rat."

I must be getting used to Nona's thrill ride because my legs didn't shake on dismount this time around. I handed Nona the helmet to hold and then walked up to the cabin. I opened the door, trying to remember what I'd seen that had caught my attention. It was a book. A library book, to be specific. I began shoving treasures to the side in order to make a trail to the table the book was sitting on. It was an old book that chronicled the colorful period in time when Ashton Falls was still Devil's Den.

There was a piece of paper stuck in toward the center of the book that acted as a bookmark. I opened to the page that had been marked. It was a story entitled *The Dollinger Gang*. I seemed to remember Suzy saying something about Pack Rat telling her the story of the Dollinger gang but not having a chance to finish it. I decided to take the book out onto the porch where the air was fresher.

I was about to leave when I noticed a photo on the wall, of a military platoon. I tucked the book under my arm and made my way toward the picture. There were twelve men in the photo, all of whom looked to be around twenty years old. I studied the faces in an attempt to pick out Pack Rat. He was much older now, and much more worn as a result of a life lived on the streets. He did have kind eyes that seemed to sparkle with intelligence, and he was tall. I studied the men in the back row until I was able to pick him out. There was a short man standing in front of him. He had both arms, but I was willing to bet that was Stubby. I'd never met the man, but Salinger knew what he looked like. Making a quick decision, I took the photo with me.

"Find what you were after?" Nona asked.

"I think so. I need to go back into town. To the sheriff's office."

"Hop on."

This time I didn't even hesitate. I found I was actually looking forward to the ride. It seemed that Zak's crazy relative was rubbing off on me. Poor Zak. The last thing he needed was for me to get any crazier than I already was.

Nona said she'd wait on a bench that had been placed under a tree on the lawn in front of the county building while I spoke to Salinger. I'd invited her in, but she'd assured me that she didn't normally associate with "the fuzz." I told her I'd hurry and asked her to behave.

This situation really was beyond absurd.

"Yeah, that's Stubby." Salinger nodded. "After I found his body and confirmed his identity I did some additional research. It seems the platoon Pack Rat and Stubby were assigned to during the war saw heavy action. In fact, Stubby lost his arm saving Pack Rat's life."

"No wonder Pack Rat felt obligated to show him around." I continued to study the photo. "You know, this man to Pack Rat's left looks familiar."

Salinger looked at the photo more closely. "Yeah, he does, but I can't quite place him."

Salinger typed some commands into his computer. A page with mug shots of tall men with dark hair appeared on the screen. He scrolled down until he pulled up a photo of the bartender who worked in the bar outside of which Pack Rat had died.

"You think this is him?" he asked.

"Yup," I said. "It looks like the same guy. His name is Chet. Or at least that's the name he's going by now."

Salinger typed in some additional commands. "The guy was the medic with the unit."

I looked at Salinger. "A medic as in a person who would know his way around a syringe? I spoke to this man yesterday. He told me that he didn't know Stubby, so obviously he lied. One of the girls I spoke to at the arcade told me she saw the guy talking to Pack Rat on the night he died. No one seems to know exactly when he died, so I'm betting that conversation was really a cover for injecting him with the air."

"Don't you think Pack Rat would have reacted if he was sitting right there on a busy street?" Salinger asked.

"I've looked into it a bit since you told me how Pack Rat died," I informed the man. "A large enough dose of air that close to the heart could result in death within seconds."

"I'll pick the guy up to see what he has to say for himself. Good work, Donovan."

I smiled. I found I rather liked this partnership we'd developed.

After saying my good-byes I left Salinger's office to find Nona standing directly in front of a sign that read DON'T FEED THE GEESE. Naturally, Nona was feeding the geese. I just rolled my eyes at her obvious attempt at thumbing her nose at the system.

"What's next?" she asked as I approached.

"I need to stop off at the library to return this book. The library is just across the way. I can easily walk. Would you like to come along?"

Nona shrugged. "Don't have anything against libraries."

"Have you always had a problem with authority?" I asked as we walked across the lawn.

"I'm not sure. I can't remember much about my life before the stroke everyone insists I had. It seems, based on what others have told me, that I had a huge stick up my keister, so I don't spend a lot of time trying to remember a woman I'm certain I wouldn't have gotten along with at all. My philosophy is just to thank the good lord for a second chance at life and embrace every moment that's been granted me."

"That's actually really nice."

Inside the library, I headed toward the counter. Happily, Hazel wasn't busy.

"Zoe, how are you? I didn't expect to see you today."

"I had a few errands. This is Nona. She's one of Zak's relatives. Sort of."

"Happy to meet you." Nona hugged Hazel. I could see Hazel was startled by the enthusiastic greeting, but she didn't say anything.

"I found this in Pack Rat's cabin." I placed the book on the counter.

"Thank you for returning it. I'd have hated to lose this one. It's filled with all sorts of local history and legend."

"The book was marked at the story of the Dollinger gang. I seem to remember that one of the merchants I spoke to this week mentioned that Pack Rat had been telling them the story but was unable to finish. Do you know anything about them?"

"Actually, I do," Hazel confirmed. "The Dollingers were brothers. They lived on the wrong side of the law for most of their lives back in Devil's Den, but they're best known for knocking off a stagecoach carrying a large sum of money between the local bank and the city. The money was never found. Some say they hid it somewhere in Devil's Den, but I'm pretty sure that must be just a story. It seems that if the money were here someone would have found it by now."

I thought about what Hazel had said. What if Pack Rat believed the story to be true? What if Stubby believed the story to be true? All of the businesses Stubby had broken into were housed in the old town. As we'd already realized, all the buildings in old town had been in existence since the time of Devil's Den. What if Stubby had found something he believed indicated that the money was hidden in one of these old buildings? He couldn't look around during the day when the stores were open for business, so he broke in at night when no one was around. He wanted to divert attention from the real purpose for his breaking in, so he made it look like burglaries.

"Do you know anything about the buildings in old town?" I asked Hazel. "Specifically, the one in which Gilda's place is located."

"A bit. What do you want to know?"

"Do the buildings along that block have basements or attics? Secret passages or some other sort of unseen locations?"

"You think the Dollingers hid the money in one of the buildings and Pack Rat somehow found that out?"

"It's a theory."

Hazel thought about it. "The block of businesses that were hit are located in a single structure that originally housed a brothel, a saloon, and a gambling hall. When Ashton Montgomery redeveloped the area he subdivided the building into six units that are currently occupied by Second Hand Suzie's, Trish's Treasures, Pam's Posies, Mountain Sportswear, Bears and Beavers, and Outback Hunting and Fishing. The store owners would know if there's an attic and, if there is one, would have access to it, I'm sure. But if there was originally an underground basement Ashton might have sealed it off when he modernized the building. Without an access point I suppose it could be conceivable that the existence of the basement would be unknown.

"So maybe Pack Rat and/or Stubby figured that out and Stubby broke into the businesses looking for an access point," Hazel realized.

"It's a theory that makes sense."

Chapter 14

"You can't be serious," I said to Zak that evening. We were sitting on the deck at the back of the house, settling in for what I hoped would be a super-romantic send-off to single life.

"I don't like it any more than you do, but if it will make my mother happy it's really a small thing." Zak didn't look convinced of his own argument, nor did he look any happier about things than I was.

"It's not like we haven't already," I blushed, "you know."

Zak's mom had insisted that it was bad luck for the groom to see the bride before the wedding beginning with the night before. Helen Zimmerman expected us to spend the night apart and had decided to stay at our house rather than the rental to ensure that we complied.

"I'll sleep at Levi's," Zak offered.

"No. I'll go to the boathouse." I sighed. I wasn't happy about this, but the whole nightmare would be over in twenty-four hours. "I'd rather go over there than stay here with the woman I could very well strangle in my sleep."

Zak kissed me. "I'm sorry. I know she's been driving you crazy. I knew she would. But she's my mother, so I can't just ignore her wishes entirely."

"I know. It's not a problem. It'll be fun to hang out with Ellie."

I called Ellie, packed a bag, grabbed Charlie, and headed to the boathouse. Ellie was waiting with a bottle of wine and a supportive smile.

"Just a few more hours," she said encouragingly.

"I know. It'll be fine."

"At least she doesn't live in the area," Ellie added. "Can you imagine if the woman lived in the same town you did?"

"Don't even suggest such a thing."

"Fortunately, ever since the Frankenbride incident your own mom has left you alone almost entirely."

"Yeah, I know she feels bad for the way things played out."

The assistant to the wedding planner Zak's mom had hired had taken a photo of me in my bra and underwear with a green moisturizing mask on my face. My frizzy hair was sloppily pulled into a topknot and I had a toothbrush in my mouth. She'd given the photo to a magazine that published it. The caption under the photo read, "America's fourth most eligible bachelor has landed himself a Frankenbride."

I was not amused.

My own mother, who had been on board with the wedding planner up to that point, had felt so bad for me that she'd gone to bat against Helen and worked it out so that Zak and I could have the simple wedding we'd wanted in the first place.

"I have to admit even I'm looking forward to this whole thing being over."

"Are you and Levi still coming with us on the trip?" Zak and I had invited Levi and Ellie to come with us to Heavenly Island. Our honeymoon was going to have a family theme anyway, and we really wanted them with us.

"I am," Ellie verified. "I wasn't sure about Levi, considering the whole job thing, but he can't meet with the head coach at State until after we get back anyway, so my sense is that he's still in too."

"I hope things work out. It will be nice to get away and get a break from everything that has been going on for the past month."

"I heard you all but solved the Pack Rat murder mystery."

"Maybe. Salinger hasn't been able to track down Chet, but one of the waitresses at the bar identified the hat that was covering Pack Rat's face as belonging to Chet. Chances are he fled the area after he heard Salinger was looking for him."

"Maybe. But maybe he's just hiding out until he can find a way to finish what he was trying to do," Ellie suggested.

"You think he's still looking for the Dollinger gang's loot?"

Ellie shrugged. "Could be."

I thought about what Ellie was saying. It made sense, but Stubby had already broken into all the buildings on the block. If there was a hidden door to a sealed basement wouldn't he have found it? Would the merchants have found it? Unless . . .

"Maybe the money isn't in the basement. Maybe it's in the mine."

"Huh? What mine?" Ellie asked.

"When Zak and I were trapped in the mine last week I remember him telling me that the mine system was quite extensive and ran all through the hills and even under the town. What if there was a mine access through the saloon? Maybe a back door of sorts? When Ashton Montgomery developed the town he would have sealed the entrance. Maybe Stubby thought he could find that access. If he was unable to, maybe Chet will try to look for another way in."

"That's a pretty wild theory and a huge long shot," Ellie pointed out.

"Maybe. But it's not impossible."

"Well, no, I guess it's not impossible. But how will you ever find this mythical access even if it does exist?"

I paused to think about it. I really had no idea. I was about to suggest a research trip when I heard a loud rumbling outside. I opened the door. It was Nona.

"What are you doing here?" I asked as she pulled up to the front door on her Harley.

"I was riding through town and I saw him. The guy in the photo you showed me. The one with Pooh on his arm. He disappeared down a manhole. Hop on. We don't have much time."

I looked at Ellie.

"This is crazy," she cautioned. "Call Salinger."

I made a quick decision and climbed on the back of the bike. "You call Salinger. Tell him what's going on. Where was this manhole?" I asked Nona.

"About twenty yards east of the old town buildings."

With that, Nona gunned the engine and took off before Ellie could reply.

The trip into town was much like every other with Nona: insane. I hung on for dear life, praying I'd still be alive to get married the following day. Nona cut the engine before we actually got to the manhole. We got off the bike and walked the rest of the way.

"Do you think he's still down there?" I asked.

"Just one way to find out." Nona turned to climb inside.

"You can't just go down there. It's dangerous. What if he has a gun?"

"You want to get this guy?"

"Well, yeah."

"Then let's do this."

Nona climbed out of sight before I could argue further. I couldn't just let her go down there alone, so I climbed in after her.

The tunnel was dimly lit by emergency lights. As I followed closely behind Nona, I found myself hoping many things. I hoped we would find Chet and I hoped we wouldn't. I hoped the rustling noises were only mice and nothing bigger. I hoped the power wouldn't go out and plunge us into darkness. I hoped Zak wouldn't be too mad, and if he was, I hoped I'd live to make it up to him.

"Why do you think he risked coming down here?" I whispered. I was so close behind Nona that my mouth almost touched her ear.

"If the sheriff questioned him, he must have realized he had to split. Probably figured this was his last shot."

"Yeah. I guess that makes sense."

"Shhh," Nona cautioned. "I hear something up ahead."

I frowned. The woman was fifty years older than me and she heard something I didn't. I hoped I was half as spry at her age.

We inched forward, one small step at a time. I could hear the sound of our breathing as we made our way deeper into the tunnel. I'd have sworn I heard the sound of our beating hearts, but I supposed that was just my imagination. We came to an intersection. Nona paused to gauge the situation. She was just about to take a step toward the passage on the left when someone plowed into her from the tunnel on the right.

I screamed.

"What the hell," Chet spat. "What are the two of you doing down here?"

"Just out for a stroll," Nona tried.

Chet shone his flashlight in my eyes. "You're that pest who's been going around asking about Pack Rat and Stubby."

"No. That's not me. Must be a pest who looks like me. Grandma and I are just doing a little spelunking."

I couldn't see Chet's face. With the light in my eyes, I couldn't see anything. Still, I was certain he didn't believe a word I said.

I caught a flash of light from what I imagined was a gun. "Both of you start walking," Chet instructed.

"You found the money," I stated.

"I might have."

"So you were in on the whole thing with Pack Rat and Stubby?" I fished.

Chet motioned with his gun for Nona and me to start walking. He followed closely behind me. Much too closely, in my opinion.

"Actually, I didn't know anything about the loot until Stubby came into the bar shooting his mouth off about it," Chet answered. I was kind of surprised when he did. I assumed his willingness to talk indicated that he planned to kill us. "After hearing Stubby's description, I realized the loot he'd been looking for was probably down in the tunnels. I could tell Stubby didn't know about the street access. When I realized Pack Rat was in the truck, I went outside and asked what he thought about the loot, and he said he thought it might be down here as well."

I stopped walking. I felt the gun being pushed into my back.

"So why didn't Pack Rat go after it?" I asked.

"Guess he didn't want Stubby to find it. Now get moving."

Nona and I continued walking slowly down the dark passage.

"So why kill Pack Rat?" I asked.

"He didn't like Stubby stealing from everyone, so he was going to go to the cops. I figured once he did, the secret would be out."

"So you inserted air into his neck?"

"It was quick and mostly painless."

Nona stopped walking this time. She turned around and looked at Chet. "You always keep syringes in your pocket?"

"It wasn't in my pocket. It was in the bar. I waited until no one was around and went back out after speaking to Pack Rat the first time."

"You keep syringes in the bar?" Nona clarified.

Chet shrugged. "I do what I need to make ends meet. Sometimes that includes dealing in black market items, including syringes. Now scoot."

When we got to the end of the passageway we turned and looked at Chet.

"What are you going to do with us?" I asked.

"I should shoot the two of you, but the old broad looks just like my own meemaw. I can't let you tell anyone you saw me until I can make my getaway, though."

Chet picked up the bags and tucked them under his arm. He motioned us toward the back of the room. "Hand me your cell phones."

We did.

Chet tucked them into his pocket and then closed the door that separated the room from the rest of the tunnel system, plunging us into darkness. My stomach lurched when I heard the distinctive clunk of the lock being pushed into place.

"I don't suppose you happen to have a flashlight on you?" I asked Nona.

"Not a flashlight."

A few seconds later I heard her strike a match. It illuminated the room, but I knew it wouldn't last long. Nona pulled a cigar out of her bra, which she promptly lit.

"You keep a cigar in your bra?"

"You never know when one might come in handy. We need something that will burn longer and brighter, though."

We used the very faint light from the cigar to look around the room for something else to burn.

"How many matches do you have?" I asked.

"Just a couple more. There's something in the corner."

I slowly crawled over to check it out. It was a burlap sack full of money.

"Looks like he forgot one."

"Money burns," Nona commented.

"It won't burn for long."

"If we wrap it up into a ball and then wrap the bag around it, we should get light for quite a while. Haven't you ever made a paper log?"

"No," I answered honestly. "I can't say that I have."

Nona made the log she referred to and then lit it with her cigar. She then paused to smoke the rest of the cigar.

I coughed. "That thing smells awful."

"Want a hit?"

Did I?

"Sure. Okay. I've never smoked a cigar before."

I placed the foul-smelling thing to my lips and inhaled. Now I started coughing uncontrollably.

"Good stuff," I said while gasping for air.

Nona laughed. She leaned against the wall and continued to smoke while our small fire smoldered.

I looked around the room. "If there isn't an air source that fire is going to asphyxiate us."

Nona shrugged. "I wouldn't worry. Your friend knows where we are. I expect Zak will come crashing through that door any minute. The boy has it bad. You've really captured his heart. He's not gonna let you die."

I realized Nona was right. Zak would come for me. He always did.

"I've been thinking," Nona casually added. "If the two of you should have a girl I'd like you to name her Emily."

"Emily? Is that your name?"

"No. It's the name of my daughter. She died when she was twelve."

"Oh, I'm so sorry." I felt my eyes tear up, although I wasn't certain whether it was from empathy or the smoke.

"She would have liked you. You've got spunk. The women Helen was continually throwing at

Zachary would have been limp noodles hyperventilating by now."

"This may surprise you, but this isn't the first mine shaft I've been trapped in. In fact, it isn't even the first one this month."

Nona laughed. "No, I imagine it isn't. You're okay, Zoe Donovan. Don't let Helen or anyone else tell you otherwise."

I hugged Nona as Zak broke down the door. Once again, my knight in shining armor had come through. As Zak scooped me into his arms, I somehow knew that as long as I continued to get into trouble he would continue to save me.

Chapter 15

The Wedding

I'm not sure what I imagined I would feel as Zak and I stood face to face and declared our love for each other in front of our family and friends. I imagined I'd be nervous and just a bit unsure. I worried that I wouldn't know how to stand or what to say. I was certain I'd have cold feet and would second-guess everything I knew to be true, but what I never imagined was how completely I'd be drawn into his gaze.

They say that when you die your life flashes before your eyes, but as I stared into Zak's eyes I saw our future unfold. The children we would raise; the adventures we'd share; the tears we'd shed, as well as the love and the laughter that would see us through. Any doubt that I'd ever had faded away as the years unfolded, and I knew that the man I willingly bound myself to was happily binding himself to me as well.

Zak's hands felt sweaty as he held mine, but I held on tight, knowing that our entwined hands represented the beginning of our entwined lives. Pastor Dan droned on as he'd been instructed to by Zak and me. I guess I must have responded appropriately, but I didn't really hear what he was saying. As I opened myself to Zak's strength, for the first time in my life I fully understood his vulnerability. I vowed in that moment to protect his heart and keep it safe no matter what the future might bring.

"Do you, Zoe Donovan . . ." Dan began.

"Wait."

I could feel everyone hold their breath at the unexpected interruption. I'm certain every guest on the premises thought I was about to run. But not Zak. I could see it in his eyes, and in that moment I knew he trusted me with his heart as completely as I trusted him with mine.

I smiled and squeezed Zak's hand as a tear slid down his cheek.

"I, Zoe Harlow Donovan, take you, Zachary Zion Zimmerman, to be my lawfully wedded husband. To have and to hold from this day forward. I promise to love you with my next breath, my last breath, and with every breath in between. I promise to be your partner in all things, as well as your biggest fan and staunchest supporter. I promise to always choose you, no matter what the choice, and I promise to bring just enough craziness into your life so that you'll never grow bored. I give myself to you completely and without reservation. I love you, and I will continue to love you every day of my life."

I had more in my heart but couldn't continue. Dan looked at Zak for direction; we'd told him we wouldn't be reciting our own vows, but he didn't respond because all his attention was on me.

"I, Zachary Zion Zimmerman, take you, Zoe Harlow Donovan, to be my lawfully wedded wife. To have and to hold from this day forward. I promise to love you with my next breath, my last breath, and every breath in between. I promise to be your partner in all things, as well as your biggest fan and staunchest supporter. I promise to always choose you, no matter what the choice, and I promise to always rescue you when your huge heart gets you into trouble. I give myself to you completely and without reservation. I love you, and I will continue to love you every day of my life."

I glanced at Alex, who stood with Bella; Scooter, who stood with Charlie; and Ellie and Levi, who stood hand in hand on the white sand beach. I knew these very special individuals would forever hold a place in my heart, and I silently committed myself to them as well.

By the time Dan pronounced us husband and wife tears were streaming down both of our faces. In fact, I'm pretty sure there wasn't a dry face on the beach.

"You may kiss the bride," Dan declared.

Zak scooped me up into his arms and held me close to his heart as we shared a kiss just a bit too long to be appropriate. Somewhere in the distant recesses of my mind, I could hear people cheering and whistling. But I didn't care. I, Zoe Donovan Zimmerman, was finally home.

USA Today bestselling author, Kathi Daley, lives in beautiful Lake Tahoe with her husband, children, and grandchildren. When she isn't writing, she likes to spend time hiking the miles of desolate trails surrounding her home. Kathi enjoys traveling to the locations she writes about to generate inspiration and add authenticity to her descriptions. Find out more about her books at www.kathidaley.com

Made in United States
North Haven, CT
30 May 2025

69362780R00114